Handwritten annotations:

To Live & Die in ~

Rabbit Fence - Australia

Chinese modernism vs U S modernism.

break up of the family -

Jane Eyre
Oliver Twist — prepare for working for families

PANDA DIARIES

Tienanmen Square - small *excuse of* revolution

a novel

What is happening
to indigenous people, is happening to animals

Alex Kuo

(signature) Margaret
Carlo -

Fledging by
Octavia Butler

University of Indianapolis Press

2006

10 Best appts of the year

Planning: Phylis Lan Lin, Executive Director, University of Indianapolis Press

Design and layout: Jeannine Allen
University of Indianapolis Press Logo: Detail from a painting by Au Ho-nien
Editors: Lauren Cragor, David L. Hanna, David Noble, R. Peter Noot
Indexer/Proofreader: Marilyn Augst, Prairie Moon Indexing

Printed in the United States of America

11 10 09 08 07 06   10 9 8 7 6 5 4 3 2 1

ISBN: 0-880938-65-X

Published by
University of Indianapolis Press
University of Indianapolis
1400 East Hanna Avenue
Indianapolis, IN 46227-3697

Fax: (317) 788-3480
E-mail: lin@uindy.edu
http://www.uindy.edu/universitypress

modernist style in writing

identity + immigration

Sherman Alexi - advisor to ←
                    Smoke Signals

1st in trilogy -

Shanghi Shanghi, Sanghi.
  relationship
Other + Self - 2 sides of one person alter/ego
  split
Human + animal

waitress in a coffee shop

1970 on west coast
Panda is a twin
Panda is a
messenger as a
mail man
  ↙ news -

55 minutes
in China

This book is for Claire,

for finding her way to cherish,

protect, and heal.

Panda/mail/man / Is the Panda real —

assimilation into Western Civilization
version of multi cultural —
parallel w/ Indians + ethnic minority in China —
Anthropologic story - Margaret Meade —
Studying humans as if they were others
- minority vs majority —
→ nation building in the name of progress

        Cultural Revolution

redwood Shemmen means " WHAT? "

        Panda is a wild animal

OTHER BOOKS BY ALEX KUO

The Window Tree

New Letters from Hiroshima and Other Poems

Changing the River

Chinese Opera

Lipstick and Other Stories

This Fierce Geography

CONTENTS

In this country the animals have the faces of animals.
Their deaths are not elegant.
They have the faces of no-one.

—Margaret Atwood
"The Animals in That Country"

I debated whether to stay in Changchun,
but it was an easy decision.
Changchun was very cold, so I moved on.

—Paul Theroux
Riding the Iron Rooster

PANDA DIARIES

PREFACE

Ruth Hackness took a deep breath and looked around, carefully marking her way through the bamboo forest deep in China's Sichuan Province. Accompanied by two American-born Chinese guides, the New York fashion designer had first sailed to Shanghai and, after 1,500 miles and five months, trekked up the Minjiang River before finally reaching these Wenshan Mountains.

A series of hesitant but hysterical cries coming from a hollow in an old withered tree froze Ruth Hackness. One of the hunters went to look. When he came back, he had in his hands a small, warm creature.

Ruth recognized it at once. "Oh, God," she said, "a panda cub."

In the meantime her husband, William, a zoologist and nineteenth-century explorer, was dying in a Shanghai hospital.

But Ruth didn't believe her luck at stumbling onto a baby panda. When she took the small animal into her arms, she felt it rub its nose against her jacket, instinctively feeling for her breast. Ruth laughed, and gave it the Chinese name *Sulin* right there, deep in the Caopo Mountains.

The adventurers took Sulin back to Shanghai by plane where they weighed and examined it at three pounds and ten days old before Ruth found out that her husband had died.

She stayed in Shanghai briefly, quickly organizing a passage back to the United States. With little trouble from customs, Sulin was smuggled out in a wicker basket labeled "Pet Dog," and docked in San Diego on Christmas Day in 1936.

Ruth was the first person to bring a panda out of China since 1869, when the French missionary Abbe Armand David acquired the West's first specimen.

For those readers who insist on a more complete sense of the historical, the linear narrative would imagine that Sulin ended up at Chicago's Brookfield Zoo, where it attracted tens of thousands of visitors until it died of an unknown disease on April 1, 1938, less than two years after its arrival, and only a few months before W. B. Yeats's death and Hitler's Stuka-bombing of Poland.

Since Henry Kissinger secretly entered the door to China's Middle Kingdom on July 9, 1971, and initiated a new chapter in Sino-US relations, China has sent twenty-three pandas as diplomatic gifts to nine countries: Korea—five; Japan—four; and the Commonwealth of Independent States, Great Britain, Mexico, the US, Spain, France, and Germany—two each.

Every year since then, whenever a Nicolae Ceausescu is not losing his testicles in his own palace; or an Imelda Marcos is not counting her missing Parisian alligator shoes; or a Prince Charles is not traversing the remnants of the British commonwealth whining about the abuse of the English language; or the Palestinian and Israeli youths are not trying to kill each other with rubber bullets, stones, or more specific targeted killings; or another still-living *Enola Gay* airman or *USS Arizona* swabby is not saluting the flag; the world media focuses on the copulation effectiveness of these twenty-three zoo-bound pandas.

The Self, the Other /+ differences

"[The Soul of the Octopus"] Book

Breaking up of Panda families

Mirroring of human + panda animals
animal is a commodity

CHAPTER ONE

Mask - what is real + what is a mask

Book is asking questions - rather than
real memories -
reality + perception -
is my truth your truth -
memory is fiction fiction is memory

The Panda mailman would stop at Colonel Ge's apartment and softly knock twice at exactly the same time every week; that is, however he knew Ge was home, be it Sunday or Thursday, morning or evening. Once Ge tried to fool him by leaving his staff car with the special red-and-black license plates at headquarters and sneaking to his apartment in a cab the night before, but it didn't fool Panda. At exactly eight o'clock the next morning, Ge heard the distinctive two light taps on the metal sheeting of his security door and, opening it, he found the slightly smiling Panda balancing his three black legs of the animal kingdom against an overflowing mailbag, knowing that none of it was for Ge.

There had never been any mail for Ge ever since he moved here more than two years ago in the fall of 1989, but Panda would nevertheless stop weekly with his quiet "Hello," and sometimes twice on the same day if he had completed his route early. They would huddle together in the dark hallway and light foreign cigarettes before moving into the living room, always talking politics, becoming the friend the other needed.

On his second visit today Panda motioned Ge into the living room without waiting for the cigarette lighting ritual. He let his empty straw mailbag slip onto the carpet and ambled to the west windows where Ge had been tending some potted plants.

"It's amazing," he said. "It's almost November and you still have fresh blossoms on these nasturtiums. Back home they'd be gone before September."

Ge lit a cigarette but didn't say anything.

"Do you mind if I tried some of these leaves?" Panda asked and pointed with his one white forepaw.

"Of course, yes. Yes, you are my history; we can't remain tribal forever. But are you sure?" he added, "I mean, don't you eat only a special kind of bamboo shoot?"

"How can you believe that? Really." Panda feigned indignation, blinking his eyes. "You're supposed to be in intelligence. You've seen me smoke. If I relied only on that silly bamboo diet, we'd all be extinct by now. That's just a story our lobbyists invent for the foreign journalists in Beijing when they have nothing else to write about."

Ge trusted the moment enough to not have to imagine that he had been here before. So he smiled and nodded. Panda munched a leaf deliberately from side to side. They looked at each other, and a picture was meant to be taken of them at this exact moment, but there was no camera here to do that.

Instead they listened to the noise of the elevator whirling down from the hallway, and Panda imagined a woman waiting in perhaps another lobby, opening and reading a letter.

Dear Ma—

My fifth-grade English teacher is helping me
write letter. She is very strict. I am learning
fast. I miss you. I want to see you. Grandma
is also very strict. She wants me to study hard.
Last night I dreamed I was a snake and did not
belong, but I did not tell her. I wait to see you
on TV. The pain never misses.

Your loving son.

The trick is to not think too much about something like this letter. Attempts to scrutinize it as a Public Security Bureau interpreter specializing in decoding such texts will most likely result in self-survival, of course, but the real message would be lost. Immediately distancing questions protect the reader: Who is the author of this letter? Is he related to Ge, maybe his son? Is he actually Ge some twenty-five years earlier, when he spent three years of his banished early teens farming among the northern Oroqen ethnic minority in the government's attempt to assimilate these nomadic hunter-gatherers into its burgeoning cash-crop economy? Who is the teacher? What is a *teacher*? Did she cross the divide as teacher and actually write the letter as she imagined her pupil must have felt? Or did she stay within the promise inscribed on her stamped and framed teaching certificate like a wedding vow that is taken for granted as stated?

Maybe it is better just to accept the letter for whatever it appears to be for the moment, even though it may lead to numbing consequences later.

Going through his official mail the next day, Ge read three letters from a young intelligence officer trained at Wuhan's academy. Ge had met him at a ministry-sponsored information-sharing meeting in the capital of the three highest security agencies of the province right after his own arrival. He remembered reading Chang's dossier—specially recruited from rural background, energetic, straightforward and ambitious, college-educated, wastes no time, single, not a party member, assigned to human intelligence, on loan to provincial government security. Ge remembered concluding after the first five seconds of looking in Chang's dark eyes that he had no sense of humor, and imagined that he would even order microphones installed in his own apartment just to demonstrate the completeness of his loyalty. After reading Chang's dossier, Ge decided that in his profession the non-party members were the worst, that they will do anything to prove their worth and further their own careers, especially those with that college degree so universally despised during the cultural savaging of the sixties in which nothing was overthrown, only maimed and left not wanting.

These progressively more excessive letters, written five days apart, asked for a meeting with the colonel-in-charge to discuss the recent and sudden wisps of classified information transcribed from eavesdropped restaurant conversations among Changchun's bridge-playing zebras and baboons. Although Chang was not sure if the origin of the intelligence was signal or human, and not sure that he wanted to intrude if the activity involved only human sources, he was sure that Ge, "as the leader of the entire security network, should be apprised of the details and take compelling action to catch and punish those responsible and therefore plug up the leak" to the animal kingdom, as was written in Chang's third letter.

The more he read, the more Ge felt irritated. Why wouldn't Chang come right out and say everything in the first letter? Why didn't he just telephone me? Did he think we had no spoken language in common? Why was he masking Jilin University intellectuals as *zebras* and *baboons*? Were there other metaphors in the letters? And as far as Ge knew, these professors couldn't even follow suit, let alone talk intelligently about bridge at lunch. Chang, the crewcut Chang, assigned to the city of Changchun—it's too bad his first name was not *Chun*.

It had never been any mystery to Ge why the Japanese had picked Changchun as their Chinese capital in 1931. Changchun, Asia's Warsaw in geographic circumstance, plumbed in turn by the Koreans, Russians, Japanese, and always the missionaries in the twentieth century, as if in retribution for having given birth to centuries of conquerors. Changchun, *Forever Spring*, not ever warm enough to have an identifiable summer, now a province of half-frozen miners and truck farmers whose language has exiled the words "choice" and "rebellion." Ge knew that this was the very reason he had been expelled from Beijing on June 5, 1989. Out of the gate of the Great Wall at Badaling along with the lepers and wolves, Ge was exiled into a northern wilderness north of North Korea formerly called *Manchukuo* and before that *Manchuria*— an irremediable province of incestuous subservience whose collective *Fuck Me, Fuck Me* willfully forgave and forgot the Japanese atrocities committed against their own in the name of science at Harbin during the 1930s. So it is, Ge thought in his moment of self-anger as he stepped off the train in Changchun two years ago, all because for one microscopic moment in his meteoric career he had not been sharp enough to answer deceit with deceit.

He was twelve and sat on the hard wooden window bench in this packed bus with sleeping bag and tin lunch box—all that he would know as his own for the next three years of his life except for the clothes on his body and the two books and willow branch he will acquire later that winter. He knew without being told that he would be gone from his parents, his school, and teachers for a very long time.

The teenaged Red Guards had stormed the school in the middle of his history class and tied the teacher's wrists behind his back before forcing him to his knees to face the class and confess that everything he had taught them were bourgeois lies. Continuing in this act of the ultimate teenage revenge drama, some of them—including classmates, now cheerleaders with red armbands, waving red banners—hung a sign around the history teacher's neck, paraded him outside past the jeering market vendors, and then made him clean their toilets.

That same afternoon they trashed the school, knocking out roof tiles and windows, tearing down posters and drawings to mix with sticks of furniture and the few books from the library shelves to start a bonfire in the street, before sealing the school gates shut with a poster announcing its official closure and banishing the remaining students and teachers to labor and political rehabilitation in rural farming collectives.

He knew it would be only a matter of time before his parents disappeared in the middle of the night. Then he too would be ordered to take his things and be herded down to the detention center at the bus depot. Known as the head of his class, he could not lie, defect, and join them. It would not be the last time in Ge's life that he would be angry with himself for being such a vulnerable target for what in retrospect should have been expected and could have been avoided.

As he sat there motionless on his wooden seat, waiting for the bus to leave town and concentrating on toughening himself, he did not know that he would never see his parents again, nor did he know that he would end up an exile, farming with the northern Oroqen people in the government's program to assimilate these nomadic hunters to agriculture and profit. He just sat there and waited, prepared to meet anything, however long it took and whatever the intensity—that was how Ge learned to see the beginning of his own story—but mostly he was trying to keep from breaking down and crying, like that classmate sitting there next to him, whom Ge could not help.

CHAPTER TWO

Ge set out after the herd on the second morning before the day had dawned, ate black bread, and made no fire, the way Paishan had taught him. It was easier tracking here in the needle-padded foothills. Twice yesterday he completely lost the hoofed prints in the flats and rocks where the wind and dust had scattered and covered them, but twice he recovered them somehow—scent or memory perhaps, same thing—down there on both sides of the new, dried-out arroyo. This was his second season with the Oroqens so he was sure that no wolf that trotted neat of foot was ahead of him. Perhaps tonight after the kill he will see and hear them, loping, sidling, ambling with their long noses to the ground, great silver lobos with fire eyes, and he will then throw them the liver first.

"You will smell them first, like bears, before you see them," Paishan told him last fall. "If you cannot smell them, they are too far to shoot, even if you see them."

And Ge had understood, from the very beginning. As he and another boy from his same history class approached the hamlet of several deerskin tents after six days of riding on buses—the two preteens the government's sole supply of assistance to mandate this northern Oroqen tribe of nomadic hunters into agricultural abundance with the surrounding clan remnants under a new red and yellow banner—Ge knew that his life would be miserable without Paishan's forgiveness and protection.

As it was, Paishan chased the government's agent back down the trail with rifle and curses.

"You carry war of mad country into foreign land, you will wake more than dogs. I know what you done, and one day you will pay for it."

He fired a rifle shot after the diminishing bureaucrat and then looked at the two boys who had by now scattered like insignificant dogs behind the nearest tent under the bluest sky Ge had ever seen.

"You two best stay; it's not good for you there," Paishan pointed his emptied single-shot deer rifle at the spot where by now the government had disappeared.

Cautious now, stepping on yellowed birch leaves, aiming to not cross back itinerant, he rounded a bend and saw—for the first time since leaving the hamlet two days ago—that sharp edge of the abrupt-sided Mountain of Peace under yet another sky of bluest blue. And lower and nearer, Ge could see three reindeer grazing away from the tree-sided hills, because he saw them in his mind first.

Ge had followed them here in his thirteenth year and asked himself if these animals knew where they'd come from, and if they had entrusted their narratives to chance. The few that had survived the plague several decades ago have been useful to the still fewer surviving Oroqens, down to the last bone and tail. Like them, Ge had in one seasonal cycle learned to balance his life with the Oroqens, saddled wholly in language, rifle, and tether.

In the early mornings when he awoke in the deerskin tent still taut with chill before that blood meridian of sun had risen, Ge would watch his breath balloon into puffs of mist and be pushed along by another behind it before it, too, dissipated into this high winter here, before the silent impatience of dogs stretching onto forelegs and, outside, the further impatience of horses whinnying, ears and withers shied without hobble or rope. Ge would look beside him at his classmate in another sleeping bag, breathing past yet another night wheezing in awful fright or bronchial shudder. Ge could see his breath rising too, but knew the boy, by each day thinner into wire and bone, without language or manner, but mostly without caring, would vanquish before spring without saying a word. The dogs turned their heads away from him too, from such substantial innocence bared.

This is a tent in a dream forward where he lies, and it does not have a door. In its place, choose an empty space for him, whether rectangle or circle, or any shape of his imagining, and he will have lived in it. His eulogy is a history of doors and passages, of light to dark, or dark to light, or those journeys in between. But there is no door to this tent.

In such early, early light a young history student has picked up a rock. He hefts its weight in his hand and, taking careful aim at a tank the color of dirt, he heaves it. It strikes the turret mount with a hollow metallic sound and bounces back into the streets. Cameras from near and far record this moment. One of their pictures will later be used to arrest him, if he lives that long.

Is this why we have walked with him through the space of the tent without a door, to see this and record it too? That student might well disappear later, depending on how far we have come, and give us an ending, a void signifying his time and his place forever. And if we've come far enough, or not nearly far enough, his mothers dressed in black would then collect his promises and gather in front of the political ministry in silent vigil.

But we are too far ahead of ourselves, of course, as reliable as our metaphors seem to be in this dreaming forward. So let's check our omissions and embellishments. There, the sun is rising unstoppable, nothing turning it back there. Here in the tent is the space belonging to the frail boy, and its deerskin walls are covered with revolutionary words in several languages written in charcoal, *THE BIRD STILL LIVES.* The only sound rising from the thronging crowd outside is an inept gasp anticipating irreversible dreams. We must move on cautiously here, renew our identities, if we are to avoid the stray lunatic endangering every species.

Then, there is that twelve-year-old boy who has been left to the side of his life, or he has left it, there's no escaping it, it's all the same in this kind of random accident. He is taking a pause here too, standing before Heihe or Bogota, while across valley or street, history is declaring its own martial laws. With some spaces still empty in our passports, there is no reason why we can't take him with us. He shrugs and asks, "Will there be the sound of gunfire where we go?"

The dreams are thickest here where there is no room for error. Even the promises that have stayed around long enough not to be noticed are beginning to fluctuate. They are all saying, Look here, Look here in as many possible voices waiting to be counted. There are no explanations, and most of the time we don't even hear them, not even their symptoms, being what we are.

Let's not lie about this. That boy inside his space in this deerskin tent is dead. His breathing had stopped in the middle of the night, and Ge could not mirror the motes of vapor rising from him in the morning. He has left his story with us.

He had also left his story with Ge. Who was to console Ge his loss, a former classmate he was not close to, but who had occupied a significant space in his life? Was he what Ge had lost?

At the funeral, Ge remembered him sitting on a bench next to childless Natall in the shelter, learning to mend a birch bark basket. Natall had tried to talk with him about other things, in a voice he had not heard her use with anyone else, not even her husband, Paishan. But the boy did not talk back, and continued focusing his attention silently on his weaving. When Natall got up to place a deerskin wrap about his shoulders in the accumulating chill, he stopped his stitching, but he did not look at her. He had not learned to accept this kind of caring. But he would not move away from her either—not until now, leaving a space in her life as well as in Ge's, one that Ge could not change or touch.

Instead, when the burial ritual was over, Ge picked up a fallen willow branch that had not been covered with dirt and took it to mark the space in his tent that his fragile friend had left.

Early next spring, government came back with soldiers in uniforms of goose-shit green, the shade of neither flora nor fauna. They had pulled and pushed a wagon slouching side to side, full of hoes, picks, shovels, and sacks filled with seed. The seed was to be dropped into the ground, "Like this," demonstrated a benign People's Liberation Army conscript with hoe and boot and a grin that Ge had never seen before. Paishan understood and looked to Ge to say nothing.

That afternoon after the soldiers had left, Paishan finished the last bottle of whiskey he had traded for with furs and antlers. Drunk, he kicked at the tools and cursed well into the night in an alien language. His wife sat looking at the tools and nodding her head, even after it was too cold to stay outside.

Survival to them meant opposite things. For him, perhaps it was a moment of dramatic display; but for Natall, it was placing one thing inside another into a secret universe of unwhisperable things. Even well into the night, after the chill had settled onto their encampment and Paishan had finally run out of drink and staggered into their tent, she continued sitting there, darkened, the soot from countless other fires deepening into her face, becoming the texture of her inheritance.

The next morning Paishan was the first one up, and shouldering everyone's responsibility, went from tent to tent shaking everyone awake.

"There is no choice," he said to the group collected by a small warming fire, looking at the pile of tools and seed still untouched but by dew, a faint gathering in the history of resistance.

"We can move back into the hills," someone muttered in his half sleep.

"How long will we last, before they catch us, or before we run out of reindeer, like before," his neighbor reminded him—one who would, if given the chance, stand there forever and talk until darkness.

"Already half of what we eat comes from the trading post," laughed someone, certain of her reportage.

"We do not have to eat that much," responded another who did not exult in such subjective exuberance, who could not accept such carnival merriment as significant reason for storytelling.

"It is still chilly, maybe we can throw tools in fire," said a constructionist, bored with their metaphor explorations.

"They will be back sooner than you think."

"Then they will be back for nothing."

"The men will be sent to jail, or worse, forced to wear those goose-shit green uniforms."

"We can make a run for it, pack up and head for the border. Even if they catch us, at least we will be free a few months longer."

"And live with the Soviets, hah!"

They had been in this exact narrative before, several times this century, and collectively knew that their language was becoming a hybrid that would inevitably betray their dissidence. Only a few, like Paishan and Natall, could still love and curse in their former tongue.

"We could spend some of that free time standing here arguing forever."

"Our hamlet could splinter again…"

"…and again and again until no one's left but this foreigner here, who is more like us than some of us," Paishan interrupted, motioning to Ge. "Already we're less than half of half of what we were in my grandparents' days."

Back drunk from the trading post late one winter night last year, Paishan threw two books into Ge's tent and said, "Here, you must study these. You have the choice not to spend your whole life here."

Ge picked up the books, in a language in which he had only known the alphabet when he was still in school. Later, he came to know them as the torn Owen Lattimore's *The Mongols of Manchuria* left by a missionary in Harbin, and the brand-new T. H. O'Beirne's *Puzzles and Paradoxes* pawned by a British sailor in Dalian, both of which he will keep along with the picture of his wife and son for the rest of his life.

Ge liked the work, under dust and sun and wind, digging past sparse weeds and picking around chalked rocks for irrigation, or sometimes riding the mottled mare and breaking her colt for wagon girth or plough collar or galloping tether under a fast sky of faultless blue.

Sometimes at the end of a day's work, villagers would gather and unfold stories well into dark by nightfire until each story retold had accrued its own significance, or none at all. Some of them had no endings, and some no beginnings. Over several cycles Ge learned the Oroqens' language, why they had moved down from the forests, the history of the reindeer herds, the disappearance into the north of a splintered tribe centuries ago, and to never, ever kill a bear or a wolf. Many centuries ago someone in this predestined clan accidentally and without malice speared and killed a sow bear while mistakenly defending a child—a terrible accident, but no healing ritual could cleanse his spirit.

They tried. The sow's bones were dried and spread out on a bed of willow branches for wind burial, and someone stayed awake constantly watching to stave off the more curious wolves. Several questionable shamans performed frenzied rituals, but they lost their permit and their names were never mentioned again. Before that winter was over, the clan was gone— gone, out of sight of bone and ice and, cursed to live with only what they could carry, they headed north on foot for the mythical linking land bridge where, it was said, it would get much colder sooner before it would be warm for them. Their name would then be forever changed to *Beiulup*, a word no one would ever pronounce correctly thereafter in any language.

One morning at the end of that first summer, the same government man and same well-fed PLA soldiers in the same goose-shit green uniforms came back mounted on burros. The men so dwarfed the burros, they had to point their toes skyward to keep their feet from dragging on the ground. A faint drift of smoke still migrated over the hamlet while the weight of the landscape shifted just a little under the harvest sun. They were pleased with the birch bark baskets filled with corn and wheat, and they were even more surprised at the irrigation initiative.

"You have surpassed your quota," government man said and smiled.

"What is quota?" someone asked impolitely.

"That is about size of bottle we drink from every night," laughed another.

Not understanding this, government man continued smiling and reached out his hand to shake Paishan's, who stood back and pretended he did not know the custom, as did everyone else. When government man extended his hand to Paishan a second time, Natall interrupted and handed him the hoe she had been leaning on and asked, "You want back?"

The men and the burros returned the next day with a photographer, more seeds, and a wagon for the excess harvest. This man, whom Paishan had scared off with curses and a rifle shot less than a year ago, unzipped his wrist case and produced a handful of small brown plastic booklets.

"Here," he said to the curious who had gathered around him. "Here are your identification cards. I will write down your names and stamp them. You will need them, and you must carry them with you at all times, especially at the trading post or at the Soviet border. And that photographer there, when he is finished taking pictures of your farming development and rural reform, he will also take a picture of you together for the national newspaper."

"What is that thing for?" Natall asked, pointing to the brown plastic ID booklets, having joined the group late.

"So people will know who you are at all times," said government man.

"But people know who I am already, and they also know who my family is all way back," Natall indicated her history with an opening sweep of both arms. "And I know who they are."

"Yes, but I don't, and those Soviet soldiers in their watchtowers up there, they don't," government man pointed to the escarpment past the Mountain of Peace in the distance.

"*Shemmer?* I know you and I know them without your cards."

It was useless. Government man persisted, and the Oroqens escaped into their silence and turned and walked away from him. Paishan sauntered over to the staked burros and urinated.

By now Ge can smell the deer ahead, a distilled acrid tang. Bellying up a talus outcropping, he mustered all the air in his lungs and yapped a shout toward them with all the power a thirteen-year-old could project. The three deer heard, flicked their ears, and turned, frozen upright, the color of stilled dirt. Carefully, with only one bullet now, Ge lay down onto some scrub oak and aimed just above and behind the lungs of the smallest antlered one, dropping it instantly down into the color of dirt.

Alex Kuo

CHAPTER THREE

Panda interrupted the documentary of his travels, which they were watching on Ge's TV, his voice rising over the narrator's. "It was a dream that would not go away."

He had always thought that what people said or did was not what they really meant, and this was exactly why he and Ge became such close friends so fast—they both believed in this, which was enough to overlook all the other insubstantial differences.

"But in my dreams," he continued, "the exact opposite is true: people said and did what they really meant."

During his world travels in 1988, Panda visited Washington, DC. Only a few *lis* from both the Holiday Inn near Dupont Circle where he was a guest, and the Arlington National Cemetery where a few selected horses were also buried, he ambled across a model cutout of a short-nosed wolf with a tablet beside it:

TASMANIAN WOLF
EXTINCT
LOST FOREVER

In 1803, when the first Europeans settled on the Australian island of Tasmania, they found an animal with a head and teeth like a wolf and striped like a tiger: the Tasmanian wolf. Believing that the wolf-like animal would eat their sheep, the settlers determined to exterminate it, and they did. The last Tasmanian wolf was seen in 1933, only 130 years after the Europeans arrived.

TAKE YOUR PHOTO with this model of a Tasmanian wolf to remind you that living things are still disappearing from the earth.

"Discouraged and perplexed, I walked around the perimeter of this national zoo asking visitors if they had seen Hsing Hsing and Ling Ling, my distant cousins."

But since they were all busy taking photographic images of those inside cages or fences and ignored Panda because he was outside that space and not where he was supposed to be, and not wearing the universal shorts and hip pouches that demanded attention, he decided to take his chances trekking down to the Chinese Embassy on Connecticut Avenue.

Ge lit another cigarette and looked over to see if Panda was still watching the program on TV.

"We are both watching this, but we are not seeing what we are supposed to see?" Panda interrupted again.

"You mean that the enactment is not true?"

"But of course not. People watching this will believe it and miss the meaning of the story, as they always do. And besides, the camera always lies.

"Here I was ambling down Connecticut Avenue as fast as I could. There was no cameraman there taking pictures, but look," he interrupted himself, "I did not smile into the lens like that idiot look-alike here. No one stopped for me, because people refused to believe what they were seeing. Maybe in Washington one has to have registered lobbyists to be recognized.

"But one driver did roll down his window and yelled out *Are you lost?* in Spanish as he sped by, laughing. This is not mentioned in this documentary. Instead, we get the chirping of birds in the Mall and a swiveling view of Abraham Lincoln sitting on his hemorrhoids."

Panda got up and switched off the TV. "Let's go get something to eat," he suggested, looking at Ge out of his benign black eyes.

"How can you get hungry from watching your own biography? All right, all right, but you must promise not to create a ruckus by ordering nasturtium leaves or fresh bamboo shoots from Shaanxi like the last time, remember?"

They turned off the lights, and Ge meticulously locked the metal-plated security door to his apartment. Used to seeing Panda as the mailman, the elevator operator did not even look up from her knitting.

To avoid stares and gasps, Ge drove them to the California Noodle Company no more than three blocks away. The waitress with the very short hair was ready for them this time, after smiling to herself when she saw Panda.

"What'll you order this time, Mr. Animal Ambassador?"

"Please don't call me that. There is a difference, you know?" Panda asked back.

The waitress smiled as if she had not understood and showed them to a table in the back.

"Here, Mr. Animal Ambassador then, *ching dzwor*, or do you need a high chair? Sorry, I couldn't help it. I saw you on TV last night, that's why I called you Mr. Animal Ambassador. Or do you prefer Mr. Marsupial, or Mr. Cute Cute?"

"That wasn't me. Can't you people tell the difference?" Panda insisted.

"I'm sorry again. I've put you back here to protect you. I can say it to you, and to him too, even though I know what he does for a living," she gestured toward Ge, but something in her voice suggested that she bore no malice. "I only joke to warm you up—it's very cold early this year in Changchun. I'll bring you some tea, and I'll make yours nasturtium," she waved her pad at Panda and left.

"She's funny," Ge said, lighting their cigarettes.

"Yes, and never apathetic. She reminds me of the woman in that photograph in your apartment, the only one you have, the one with the boy."

"How do you know that?" Ge was perturbed that he had not noticed everything.

"I'm the mailman, the mailman, remember? From the mail people get or don't get, I know everything. I know what people know. I also know what people don't know but think they do."

That photograph in his apartment, the only one that Ge had besides his own in his numerous identification cards, captured a boy and a woman who looked like she might have well been his mother, but not quite willingly, leaning a bit away from him, ready to make a mad dash away from him or from the photographer, or perhaps from a distortion of the lens, or in the slightest anticipation of the camera's flash. And taken by whom—the father/husband Ge?

Are there escaped monkeys in the Washington National Zoo? The Golden Lion Tamarinds were purposely released. One gets the pleasure of seeing beautiful monkeys without bars of mesh between you and them. One learns how better to reintroduce zoo-born animals to the wild. Golden Lion Tamarinds reintroduced into Brazil by NZ staff have survived and raised babies. This is one way zoos are helping to save endangered species.

Why don't they head for the hills? Or Connecticut Avenue, like Panda? This family has everything it needs right here. Plenty of water, a familiar nest box that provides shelter and security, and each other. Why should they ever want to leave?

But just in case, if any of them are up to their monkey tricks and wander off, we can always find them. They have been belled. Around their necks are collars with miniature radio transmitters. We have special radio receivers that allow us to find each monkey by listening for the *beep...beep... beep...*of its transmitter, even when they are hiding in the Coleman cooler by Hsing Hsing, Ling Ling, or Cute Cute.

Panda had always wondered why people called some dreams *nightmares*, when most of the time they happened during the day, sometimes under the direct midday sun in the name of Fahrenheit or Celsius. Perhaps calling these acts nightmares pushed them to the side of their lives, as if they had not happened at all, so they can be ignored by historians like Arthur Schlesinger or Stephen Ambrose.

Thinking like this, did he lose his way on Connecticut Avenue? Was he darted and then given artificial respiration by an alert Eagle Scout on holiday? Or was he killed by the Park Service rangers patrolling the Mall and then stuffed and sent to the Smithsonian as a model for aspiring taxidermists?

The waitress came back with their tea, green for Ge and nasturtium for Panda. It being Sunday, the thronging crowd of families outside was beginning to gather inside the restaurant to get a closer, better stare. There had been six revolutions in Beijing this century to end feudalism, graft, corruption, nepotism, zoos, and just plain old stupidity. But apparently their news had never reached Changchun or Brevet General George Armstrong Custer in the previous century either.

All this for a bowl of noodles and cup of nasturtium tea?

Two years before Custer finally got his, just before the nation's one hundredth birthday at the Battle of Little Big Horn that was to change the colonial-native narrative forever, his boss General Phil Sheridan tried to coax the Texas legislature into creating a fellowship program to reward those hunters aiming to obliterate the Plains Indians' bison commissary. He had suggested that bronze medals accompany such endowment grants from Austin, struck with a "dead buffalo on one side and a discouraged Indian on the other." These hunters had done more in two years in settling the Indian problem than the entire regular army in thirty, he said.

Some of those who listened to him were parents themselves, and wondered about the chances for their children.

Such extravagant and indiscreet stories from the eighteenth century! First there was Mozart. Was he poisoned? White arsenic powder? Cyanide? Has his body in Vienna ever been exhumed to reveal the exact cause of his premature death? And who really cares?

But there are those naturalists, eventually proving that they too were good ol' boys, their specimen-gathering scientific rationality short-circuited by their anthropocentric will to kill just for the hell of it. Such wanton killing by Europeans in the new, new world—since the rest of Europe and Asia had already killed everything on their continents long before the obligatory compensation of Wordsworth and Coleridge, Emerson and Disney—is an impulse that has not yet seen its final day.

John James Audubon—adorning the present banner of conservation along with Aldo Leopold, Tom Regan, Jane Fossey, and Wes Jackson, too—counted in the fall of 1813 near Louisville (and he at least should be able to reliably count birds) 1,150,000,000 passenger pigeons eclipsing the sun in just three short hours alone. Even *he* believed that hunting and poisoning these same passenger pigeons would not lead to their eventual extinction, least of all long before the possibility of a civil war in the newly minted United States ever occurred to anyone.

It was not a matter of habitat encroachment that extinguished these pigeons or bison, but hunting—if not then a god-given right, at least a republican right scaled right down to the last corner of every section in every township and range, an impulse to kill everything that moved in the new world that had not stopped twitching, especially on Connecticut Avenue. They had their lights shot out by hunters long before their habitat was lost.

This was the cold war's nineteenth-century franchise in North and

public & private memory

South America, a metaphor for capital punishment, the right to expansion and the right to kill everything in its way. Shoot the reindeer in order to kill the Oroqens. Shoot the student with the poster on every continent in order to stop the revolution. These were words and phrases not meant literally, because what they said was not what they meant. But when this language appeared on the legislative floor, to its rolling block .44-90 Remington point-blank victims, it made all the difference. This uncontrollable ambiguity physically killed the body on both sides of the metaphor.

Whose nightmare was it? Who had the ammunition, and who was the rifle pointed at? In the twinning of this metaphor, every half included another surrogate from the animal kingdom, always. Count them, count them all, damn it. (See "The Animal Grammar" at the end of this novel.)

It is no wonder that some frontier parents killed themselves here where lives and deaths meant so little—they could not bear to continue being witness to this slaughter narrative they could not stop. Tears may have shimmered here and hung a moment, but they left no trace, except a transparent brittle streak down the cheeks, seen up close.

The lord is our shepherd, and were it not for random providence, we could all be sheep and be led away to slaughter.

Luck of the draw

"So that's why you are in my story?" Ge asked, when the waitress brought their noodles and coriander and cabbage and large mushrooms quick-fried in sesame sauce.

Ariel — major historian

"You're something else, Ge. You're not interested in how a giant panda bear got here, but you want to know my reasons for being here and their implications. Anyway, it's not just your story—we are in the same story. Some, like Will Durant, have just ignored our part in it because we don't speak your language, wear your apparel, or use your shelter or logic. I am not a messenger, nor is my presence a message." Then she added, nodding at the food, "Please eat before it gets cold."

"Yes, but you like our cooking, don't you, and isn't that a form of shelter," Ge asked, picking up his chopsticks.

Detecting a defensive change in his friend's tone of voice, Panda trimmed the edge from his own. "Yes, of course," he said and smiled, which was easy for him, until he heard the inept voices of the thronging crowd behind him.

In a country in which laundry detergents are sold by names from the animal kingdom—*Panda, White Cat, Goldfish*—and washing machines by flower names—*Narcissus, Lotus, Daffodil*—anything can and does happen.

For the giant panda, its namesake sells anything from razor blades to cars to bubble gum, and everything from National Football League teams to motorcycles to Kevin Costner in the second half of this double header. For one *fen* each time the name is used, its accumulated account can repurchase the Louisiana Territory with Hong Kong thrown in by 1996, or pick up the annual tab that modern China spends on banquets for its foreign guests every year.

"Here they come now," the waitress with the short hair said, "the inept gathering throng."

"Alien, alien, eating noodles, noodles, look, look, look," Panda mimicked the staring squad, until a little shit whose parents must have thought him cute aimed a black plastic AK-47s and its endless supply of clack-clack-clacks at him.

"You know, this is a replay of what happened at the Chinese Embassy in Washington two years ago—that is, after they were done laughing at me as a midget in a Halloween costume first. Here came the brat of someone with diplomatic immunity on his way to the national zoo with his plastic M-16 when he saw me first in the embassy compound. He shot me right there, his own country's gift to the rest of the world. I was quite lucky to get out of there alive."

"Maybe you should change into your mailman uniform," the waitress suggested.

"*Shemmer?*"

"Find a taxidermist to give you a suit made from human skin, huh?"

No one in the crowd laughed, but the suggestion of a uniform gave Ge an idea. He stood up to his full height, and with his long hair, he stood a figure immersed in authority and immense dignity learned from living with the Oroqens for three years. He slowly removed his overcoat. The Ministry of Public Security's deep-green uniform with the colonel's epaulets of three silver stars over a pair of braided red stripes brought the message of this century's six revolutions home to this Changchun gathering—crowd control by intimidation and mask of threat.

Using donations from the World Wildlife Fund to bell the pandas, supply them with arrow bamboo shoots in time of drought, prompt them with darts loaded with sexual stimulants and black and white compromising pinups of Rita Hayworth and Don Ameche to increase their sexual activity, the Ministry of Forestry started a campaign in the early 1980s to save the panda. In addition to using heavy earth-moving equipment from the Soviet Union and the USA—leftovers from all the wars of attrition against a receding nature—to construct protective corridors linking isolated habitats, the program also deployed French helicopters, Israeli dart guns, Japanese camcorders, South African infrared scopes, and 30,000-*yuan* Nagra miniature recorders from Sweden that could pick out a fly buzz from fifty feet, tested during the 1983 invasion of Grenada.

Using techniques developed by the Craighead brothers in their study of the Yellowstone grizzly in Montana, these eighty-five panda rescue teams' efforts were monitored from the air by representatives from the United Nations, accountants from the World Bank and International Monetary Fund, and always two cadres from the State Statistics Bureau, in addition to being filmed by ABC's David Wolper looking for another *Roots*. Using somewhat hesitant and hedging language, the national news agency Xinhua described this project with the headline, "It seems only man can save the giant panda."

CHAPTER FOUR

Ge's parents had tried to keep their lives simple. Born in 1930, Lao Xiu was too young to have fought in the revenge war against the Japanese Imperial Army and simultaneously the inherited war against the Kuomintang's mercenaries before Peanuthead Chiang Kaishek's eventual defection to Taiwan. By the time China entered the Korean War, his wife, Angli, was expecting their first and only child. His nation's obsessive haste to take the great leap forward into history by inventing its own grand narrative did not compel Lao Xiu to queue up at the neighborhood military recruiting station—he was happily married and found teaching physics at the high school very challenging and satisfying.

Angli was the new physician at the neighborhood clinic, but even so she was well liked and trusted. By the time she could not hide her pregnancy any longer, it amused her that everyone in her part of town would try to take care of her. She did not resist it but openly took pleasure in it. Crowds would part for her at the usually jammed open market, nurses at the clinic would help her down the stairs, and visitors would call at her home with eggs, milk, or the reddest river carp. Some were former patients whose names she remembered, others only their illnesses she had cured.

When they were at home alone, Lao Xiu would fill their rooms with incessant chatter and constant attention. Sometimes he would bring home something extra to cook for her, or he would fetch her another pillow and read to her from the newspapers, or spend hours washing and cleaning virtually everything in their small apartment—clothes, furniture, even the walls and outside glass that had never been touched in the two years they had lived there. During the last month he sat down one evening at the kitchen table after she had gone to bed and, in the dim light by the stove, composed what would be the only poem he wrote in his life—a love poem to her—but he waited until the morning to give it to her at breakfast.

Reading it that next morning, Angli said to him, "*Wo ai ni* forever for this," with such emphasis that neither one would ever forget.

When Ge was born that winter, both Angli and Lao Xiu vowed that they would not spoil him the way they had seen all of modern China treated by family, friends, and even strangers in the streets. Instead, they wanted to give him choice, accountability, and personal dignity, and hoped that the new country would give him a chance equal to the one they had. Happiness and dreams were never mentioned.

In Beijing in 1949, nothing else seemed to matter. After banishing the Kuomintangs to Taiwan island where Madame Chiang would again victimize the resident population, Mao Zedong spent that summer in Beijing thinking about quitting smoking, learning to substitute grace for his sluggishness, scratching his initials on the dust of every one of Beijing's forty-nine trolleys and five buses, and writing innumerable poems that an aide copied, saved, and later published in several languages. But mostly he avoided comrade Zhou Enlai's ever-pressing question, *What are we going to do now?*

But on October 1st of that year, he was a monument there on Tiananmen Square between the Temple of Heaven and the Forbidden City, facing south in the tumultuous afternoon sunlight, the entire city thronging with millions of red and yellow chrysanthemums and their accompanying yellow jackets. Caught between Edward Murrow, Movietone cameras and BBC microphones, Mao said to himself in the past perfect tense of Chinese grammar, "This is it."

On October 1st of that year, Lao Xiu was a senior at Beijing's Qinghua University, which had been reestablished under the direction of the psychologist and educator Z. Y. Guo, experienced in keeping institutions running and classes open in both war and revolution. Lao Xiu took time off from writing his thesis and joined some of his classmates in the thronging crowd in front of the review stands downtown on Tiananmen Square. In such an intense moment of optimism projected into that early October afternoon in the center of the center of the Middle Kingdom, he too wanted to believe that everything will be all right, that given the right effort, everything will be given a reasonable chance, however difficult.

At least Lao Xiu and Angli had been exiled together, rounded up by loyal cadre members in the middle of the night and the middle of the cultural dissolution, and sent to a remote agricultural village in Yunan to be reeducated in the fundamentals of socialism by working as extra field hands. Just moments later, their son Ge would be ordered onto another bus in the opposite direction, to do the same among the Oroqens. This is where 800,000,000 other Chinese live and die every year. This is also where Chang was raised and why he was especially recruited for spying on his neighbors; its shadows and echoes he would spend the rest of his life desperately shaking off.

cultural revolution

On this half-day of rest Lao Xiu and Angli squatted in the sunlight outside their one-room hut, which they shared with another exiled couple from a coastal city. It was one of the few days in their lives at the village they could remember feeling unthreatened by sky, wind, or politics. They were reading the remnants of a two-month-old newspaper that had found its way to the village wrapped around a kerosene lamp. All morning long their lips had been tightly closed, but Angli leaned her head against Lao Xiu's shoulder as they both peered into the announcement that the county government had organized reading classes in all of its villages in an aggressive campaign to wipe out illiteracy nationally.

"So it's true," Lao Xiu said, fitting two torn pieces of the newspaper together.

"Yes, but what will come of it? Learning to read at the consumer level to expedite the grading of grains, eggs, and meat?"

"But it's a start."

"Literacy as filling a quota report without being cheated by the middleman? Or learning the trick of passing on the usurious interest?" Angli shifted a little and stared at a spot on the ground.

"You didn't hear neighbor Ah Q two nights ago, you had fallen asleep," she continued, picking up a stick and drawing designs in the dried dirt in front of her feet. "He was yelling at his daughters again. He forbade them to attend these reading classes and said, 'Sitting out there in the evening air, feeding mosquitoes, it's a waste of time. I will not permit you to go.'"

There was a stir down by the melon patch where several villagers had gathered. The crowd was getting larger, with shouts, nervous laughter, encircling something that Lao Xiu and Angli could not see clearly above the stirred dust and waving sticks.

By the time they got there, someone had tossed a firecracker at the two captured white cranes in the circle, and the sudden pop made both the crowd jump back a little and the cranes jerk their necks tighter against the already taut line holding them back. A small boy was darting in and out of the adults, poking a sharp bamboo stick at the cranes' long legs where some skin was beginning to parch and flake off.

"Why are they doing this?" Angli wanted to know.

"Yes, why are they?" A wandering monk in a flowing long orange robe appeared beside her and greeted her with his hands together, fingers lightly touching.

After Angli and Lao Xiu returned his greeting, the monk turned aside and extended the same greeting to the man holding the line taut, the proud jailer of these prisoners from the wild animal kingdom. The noise in the crowd was beginning to subside, and the buffoon smiles slowly replaced by something resembling guilt.

"These are holy creatures, my man, they are messengers from the sky," he said.

"Some depend on them for their lives," he added, but only Lao Xiu and Angli caught his double meaning.

"Yes, yes, I have heard," the man with the line said, but he was already beginning to release the tension that tied him and the village to the two cranes.

"So why have you captured them, and allowed them to be teased and tortured?"

"We are very poor here. I can bring much money by selling them to the zoo in the city there," he waved his fist with the lines at something in the valley down below them, in the process jerking them tighter against the cranes' necks again.

"How much do you think they will give you?" the monk asked.

For the first time that afternoon the villager with the cranes started to look serious, took his time, and began adding everything together, the eyes of the entire village watching his calculations.

"Perhaps 200," he finally said, forty centuries of bartering experience in his voice.

"That's outrageous," interrupted Lao Xiu.

"Sh, sh," the monk said to him. Then he turned to the man with the cranes. "I'll give you 400 for both of them, *hao ma?*"

"Where did he learn to haggle, in a temple?" Angli said to her husband.

The man with the cranes started to pull up on the lines again, the furrows over his dusted brows accentuated in the afternoon sunlight. Perhaps he had made a mistake and underestimated their worth. Everyone was quiet again, motionless, looking at him, until the monk walked over to him before he could change his mind.

"Here's the money," he said, tucking the cash into his fist and taking the lead lines away from his other hand.

"Where did he get all that money?" someone asked.

"I thought monks were always poor," another one said.

"I heard that monks always have lots of money," another shook his head.

Before the man with the 400 *yuans* in his hand could recover, it was already too late. The cranes were already in the air, released by the monk, their long legs tucked into their line of purposeful flight, white wings pulsing toward the north away from them, perhaps in the direction of Hiroshima where, according to legend, a young victim on her final threshold waited to see them from a hospital bed before she was willing to die.

The annual flood came early every spring. Every year at about the same time, all the villagers would leave with everything valuable that they could carry, haul, pull, or push, while the river surged above its waterline and mapped its way through the village. Every year the villagers would return with more things than they had left with in about two or three weeks and begin cleaning and rebuilding, longer and with still more things if the previous winter had left a heavier snow pack.

At one point in the village's history, there was talk of trapping the Floodwater Deity with a net made of every thread in the village and casting it across the river at the height of the flood, anchoring one end to the giant banyan at the bend in the river just above the village. If they could only trap the Floodwater Deity, haul it out of the muddy water and let it dry in the air and sunlight for three consecutive days, then the floods would cease forever and never again devastate the village. But at that time there was no one in the village committed enough to organize this effort, and not everyone was willing to sacrifice every piece of thread, rope, string, yarn, twine, animal hair, and lint for something that they were not so sure about. They knew they would at least eventually use that last piece of saved string, if only to tie some duck's legs together for the market.

In the end someone muttered that it was a good thing that they did not kill the Floodwater Deity, since the end of floods would also mean the end of rain, the end of crops, and the end of their way of life. So every spring since then there has been the flood, something they could count on running away from, and a few weeks later they would return again to the exact same spot in the landscape to rebuild whatever the river had taken, before they put in their new crops, before the river would take them away again next spring. It had not occurred to them to move back somewhere else away from the river; and it did not occur to the Ministry of Agriculture to control the river until an exchange student returned from America in 1981 with several manuals from the US Corps of Engineers on how to wage war against nature as it had against the Atchafalaya.

Upon returning with the villagers after their first spring and first flood in the village, Lao Xiu said to Angli, "I used to think that storytellers had to be survivors, but I've changed my mind. They can tag someone to do it for them, provided they choose the right person. Look at that one over there," he pointed to a neighbor who was just putting the final bricks to his hut's only window. "His face is full of shadows and echoes, he's the professional storyteller here. All he has to do is just repeat everything that's been given to him in the right sequence. He doesn't have to understand a word of it, not one, the maggot."

"I know, I know, but I'm not sure I can go through another one of these evacuations," Angli replied, her back aching from raking the debris around their hut. "It's a double evacuation for us, you know. When the flood is over, we come back to the same thing—we are still in the evacuation, we are still the same displaced persons paying the penalty for an unknown crime. The price of kerosene keeps on going up, Ah Q complains, like he complains about what children today are coming to, like he complains about the mobile United Nations activist interfering with the village's cranes, but he sees these repetitions as annual renewal rites rather than death."

They looked at each other. For the rest of the day they did not say anything. Like two persons very much in love, their silence told them everything each needed to know.

It was bitterly cold that winter, accompanied by a heavy snowfall. The villagers spent most of their time keeping themselves warm and chopping the few remaining dried stalks and husks left over from the corn and wheat harvest into feed for the hogs, livestock, and the few chickens that they had brought into their huts. It was the only time that everything in the household came close to being equal—the women did not have to wait for the men to finish eating and leave the hut before they'd pick up their chopsticks, and everyone washed out of the same cold water in the shared basin that the chickens drank from, and nobody used the shared mirror hanging over the shared stove.

It was the only time that some people like Ah Q got a chance to recognize whom he had in his own family, rather than pairs of hands that could or could not do the work quota in the fields.

The villagers could see it coming, inch by inch for several days that spring, there, the river carrying with it as flotsam lumber from the huts of the upper villagers, an occasional bloated goat, or suckling pig browned and drowned by the muddy water.

Then last night Lao Xiu and Angli could hear the flood getting stronger and closer, feeling it change the bend in the river above the village into an island. While their neighbors were scurrying about collecting all their belongings and yelling at them to do the same, they sat down by the shared table in their hut, and Lao Xiu filled their kerosene lamp with the reserve tin under their cot.

They had talked it over before now, and were prepared to stay. But they wanted to write a letter to their son Ge, not knowing where he might be.

"How can this be done?" Lao Xiu asked.

Angli continued looking down at the ink she was muddling. She could have had that look that night, or any other night since their arrival at the village.

"How does one write a parting letter from one generation to another?" he asked again.

"We must be honest," Angli said and looked up at him, her eyes as dark as the ink she was making. "We must tell him that life is not worth living anymore for us."

Xiao Gee—

We don't know if you will ever read this last letter from us—we don't even know where they have sent you or if you are still alive. Your mother is at the table with me, preparing the ink.

We are at the frontier here; our lives are being re-directed. But we are too old to just make do and endure the present for another five years, and another five years after that in a program of planned progress drawn by old war horses.

We don't have that much forgiveness left in us either; and we don't have that much luck or strength anymore.

We refuse to bleed for the right to live in a war of attrition against what we believe in. And we refuse to continue living a life in which nothing heals, and where life counts for so little.

We hope you have endured, and have found something worthwhile to inherit from our lives, and our choice to die.

Several years later when Ge was about to take his university admission exams, a distant relative found him one night poring over probability tables and gave him this old letter.

After he read the letter, Ge started reciting to himself the numbers he knew best, 1, 3, 5, 7, 11, 13, 17, 19, 23, 29, 31, 37, 41, until he reached identicals in their higher alignments before he could look up again.

It's difficult to maintain one's safe neutrality when Lao Xiu and Angli have left us within the folds of their own bodies. But we must remember that we are of infinite kin, and like their son Ge, we must find a way out of the murk in this alien country, war or no war.

CHAPTER FIVE

Who is Chang?

Ge woke up a good half hour before the sunrise, a cold red haze that he watched from his kitchen window. Then he remembered his meeting later that morning with Chang, and with that, the question surfaced again. On this, the dossier did not offer up much for interpretation: place and date of birth, university marks, rank in espionage school, location and length of previous assignments, the same numbers that could appear under the name of almost half the case agents in the ministry, and available to anyone with only a general access code to a computer. Ge wanted to know more: if Chang had been a typically spoiled child who shared nothing, if he liked oral sex or had a sex life at all, if he had any friends who were non-party members, or if he hated Changchun.

We are so cautious and secretive that we keep secrets from each other. I can find out more about the dedicated Chang whom I don't trust by going to a bank and looking at a copy of his loan application, something a foreign agent or journalist or Lonely Planet travel guide editor can also do. I am in charge of security here, and I can't find out any significant information on someone who works several levels below me, someone who has written me three times in just one week requesting a meeting with me over something approximating our national security. How can I take any responsibility? Or is that the point? Was that the real issue at Tiananmen Square?

Ge shook himself out of it, and at seven o'clock exactly, just as a flight of five pigeons fluttered by his window, his telephone rang. It was his son Xiaoyao with a reverse charge call from his grandparents' home in Shanghai, every third day at this prearranged time.

The two of them took to the west on horseback, curried and long-legged and without bit, avoiding towns and cities, across open country. They slept outdoors and did not tire. They risked the truth and spoke to each other clean and honest, without being asked, all the way down to blood and bone, what they owed each other a generation apart three days later.

Ge had decided to leave his staff car with the white plates and red GA and black numbers at the apartment and walk the cold distance to the office downtown. He suspected that he had to give Chang his full attention, and wanted the time to prepare himself for it.

Chang came in calling "Colonel leader, Colonel leader," his eyes searching for two possible exits from the office, like he was trained. Ge had not been mistaken about him.

The room was empty. The vaults and abacus had been put away. There was no one else there, no one for Chang or for him to suspect. There was only white, empty space.

The bicycle barely missed Ge, distracted by his dreamwalk, paying attention to the wrong details.

Too close. Run over at that speed on a racer, I would've been smushed, the first bicycle fatality in human history, hah, hah, narrow loam marks ribbed across my forehead, tulips on my belly. What would Paishan say, hah, hah. How fast does Xiaonyao ride his bike? Oh, oh, does he wear a helmet?

Eight o'clock, and the Baihan work unit bus is late again. The buildings loom nearer, now Stalin Boulevard. Perky short hair, just washed this morning, cute moves, Han nationality and married. The middle glass door here, opened for me, thank you, Wang, out of the cold quicker. You've cut yourself shaving below your lip the second time this week, but you better check my pass, badass cadre. Look closely, see, I might be a spy, hah, hah, were the truth be known.

Ni hao?	*Ni hao.*
Ni hao!	*Ni hao.*
Ni hao.	*Ni hao!*
Ni hao!	*Ni hao?*
Ni hao.	*Ni hao?*
Ni hao?	*Ni hao!*

Wo bu hao, and fuck you. Good, eight-thirty, an hour before Chang shows up. Maybe he's here early? Let's see what provincial secrets they want me to have a need to read this morning.

There is no graffiti at the urinals at the bus depot or student dormitories. In China there is no graffiti, except occasionally on the walls of Tiananmen Square. But there is a new sign, here at the men's washroom on the second floor at the headquarters of Jilin Province—National Security Building, a reminder to all the men on the go:

No Prostitution
No Gambling
No Licentious Behavior
No Uproarious Noise
Do Not Move Furniture
Do Not Flush when Done
You're Standing on It

To market, to market, an on-site investigation into signal intelligence leaks most probably involving human sources unearthed by citizens alerted to the dangers of leaks that threaten the national security.

> Four Ugandan chimpanzees smuggled to the Soviet Union last year have been returned home after an international campaign to rescue them, a mobile United Nations official said on condition of anonymity in Kampala on Sunday.
>
> Ugandan wildlife officials said the four chimpanzees—three males and one female—were exported in a secret deal between government officials and a foreign trader that would have swapped the primates for prisoners of war and a Siberian tiger of either sex.

Across People's Square go Chang and Ge on foot to the open market where someone two weeks ago had discovered some trashed computer printouts outlining the People's Liberation Army's air squadron command structure, with officers' names, addresses, and telephone numbers in Changchun, a definite security violation that had to be stopped, explained Chang for asking for this morning's meeting. Several blue-suited older men in matching Mao hats were walking around the square exercising their song birds in the −14° Celsius temperature, gently swinging their cages of finches, warblers, and parakeets of insubstantial bone. These birds have been domesticated for more than twenty centuries, but the owners in today's China are mostly fewer and older and retired, the rest lost to the modern wars or victims of suicide during the cultural dissolution of the sixties.

"It's 220," Chang said, unfastening the top button of his tunic uniform.

"*Shemmer?*" Ge asked, even though he knew what the number meant. Numbers have always stayed with him, ever since he entered the world of mathematical language in the three years that he spent living with the Oroqens as an early teenager. But knowing that he and Chang were going to be together today for a long time, Ge tried to make his patience last by adopting a humorous perspective for himself in feigning this ignorance.

"The printouts were found in the gutter behind Stall 220," Chang answered, looking at Ge suspiciously.

"Yes, yes, of course, Number 220." Ge offered Chang a cigarette, which was refused.

He probably doesn't drink either, except maybe at Deng Xiaoping's birthday party, or eat pork—a Muslim fundamentalist, good background for espionage recruitment. Perhaps the ministry did do something right for a change. But does it mean that at noon every day he'd quietly have to slip out his kneeling mat and face west and pray to Mecca? Interesting problem. If he had to, which would he choose: his country or his religion? Maybe one day someone would ask him to prove his loyalty by shooting a couple of his own men, hah, hah. That's been done before in Changchun, in the 1930s during the Japanese occupation.

In front of Stall 222, an early shopper was haggling with the seafood vendor over the price of a duck flapping its clipped wings, its neck stretched and hanging from the grasp of the owner holding it at arm's length for show.

"Here, feel it, feel it, feel how fat it is," he demonstrated, pinching the duck's stomach below the down folds. "It's worth it."

When the shopper removed the glove from his right hand and made his pinch test, the duck defecated and flapped its wings faster, managing at the same time to emit a shortened *quack*, its throat clutched tight in the owner's fist.

"But it's not very obedient," he said. "For that price, it should be able to sing."

"What does obedience matter when you're going to eat him? I'll show you," he continued, releasing his hold on the duck's neck in order to free both hands, grab it around its body, and slap its head against the corner timber of his stall. Whack! The duck stopped flapping its wings and settled down, its eyes glazed the color of isinglass. The owner then placed the duck down in front of the shopper's feet, where it remained motionless, almost asleep, its feet double looped in twine.

In the square outside a deteriorating Buddhist temple overhung with vines somewhere in neighboring Thailand, a small boy squats and talks in a low voice to the several birds he keeps locked up in a rattan cage in front of him. For the right amount of tourist money, he will thumb open the latch of the gate and release a bird in flight.

After the tourists leave, the birds will fly back into the cage of their dependency.

Chang was doing all the asking.

"How did you get this paper?" he questioned, his voice full of intimidation, pointing with his single sheet of computer printout.

The fish seller of 220 was beginning to show nervousness. He looked at the perforated computer paper and then at Chang's uniform. It wasn't exactly the uniform of the Public Security Bureau of the province or city, but it was imposing enough, especially with the epaulet bars and stars. Ge he wasn't sure about, though he looked distant and obviously in charge, and through experience knew him as the type who will seriously repeat the exact same questions later. If he told lies now, he had better remember what they were so he can repeat them exactly later.

"I bought it last week, from the junk man," he said. "Here, I'll show you." He lifted the counter lid to his stall and produced a small stack of used computer paper from the corner where he kept his weighing scale, knocked off Texas Instrument calculator, twine, and old newspapers.

"What's this? You have more?" Chang picked up the stack and examined them. The partially ripped top set listed the PLA air squadron stationed at Changchun's forty-year-old Korean War vintage warhorse, MiG-15s by serial number, their dates of production and purchase from the Soviet Union, and their maintenance records.

"Look at this," Chang showed Ge the papers. "This is highly classified information, a severe breach of motherland security."

While Ge flipped through the papers, Chang asked the vendor, "What are you doing with this?"

The fish seller looked confused. He didn't understand the question but didn't want to appear impertinent by asking. He was desperately trying to guess what the question meant so that he could provide the correct answer.

"It's for customers to wrap fish with," he finally tried the truth, hoping that it would work.

Chang looked at Ge, but Ge was pretending to be occupied by the print-outs. Instead, Ge was thinking how much Chang loved his work, how he was making love to it right here in the open market in front of a gathering crowd.

"That doesn't sound right at all, not at all. Let's see all your identity cards," Chang ordered.

The fish seller reached into his belt wallet and produced them: laminated license for the stall with photo, laminated certificate of tax stamp with photo, brown unit booklet with photo, black resident booklet with photo, red special merchant purchasing booklet with photo, white merchant traveling permit booklet with photo, and green permit to make Foreign Exchange Currency transactions, with photo, all officially stamped and current.

Chang meticulously checked each one, and then handed them to Ge, who was still pretending to examine the printout sheets.

"You have one missing here," Chang said.

"No, no, they are all here." He was clearly worried.

The thronging crowd shifted and started to move away a little.

"Where is your swimming identification?" Chang asked, looking at the fish seller straight in the eye.

The crowd moved farther back. The fish vendor in the neighboring stall looked panic-stricken, ready to make a bolt for it.

"*S-S-shemmer?*"

"You handle fish, don't you? You must have a valid provincial swimming identification card."

"Chang," Ge interrupted quietly, his finger beckoning Chang over.

"What's this," he whispered. "There's no such thing as a swimming identification card."

"Yes, yes, you know that, and I know that, but he doesn't," Chang pointed at the fish seller. "There's a major security violation here, and he must be punished."

As someone who had refused to use commonplace deceptions or trucked-in hegemonic codes in his own life and at work through his entire career, Ge raised his head, brought his shoulders back and looked deep into Chang—the exact same look he gave Comrade Marshal Zhao when he was asked on the political evening of June 4, 1989, if he could assess the damage and provide an accurate body count on both sides of Tiananmen Square.

Chang took down the name of the junk man, a Li Pengzhi, and on the IBM computer back at headquarters accessed his address, a low number on Dong Zhong Hua Lu with the exclusive 82 telephone prefix. Caught up in a crossed signal and human intelligence investigation he could find no appropriate excuse to exit, Ge drove with Chang to the neighborhood of the 1930s Japanese-built formal houses with courtyards now turned into vegetable gardens, reserved mostly for retired high-ranking provincial officials. Chang parked the official car two blocks away.

"Pretty fancy for a junk man—a front for the CIA, KGB, MI-6 or the Mossad perhaps? How can he make so much money from buying and selling junked paper, glass and metal—you tell me," Chang asked, picking the lock to the unattended house. "Pretty clever," he added, "pretty clever front."

While you're at it, Chang, why not Mitsubishi, Exxon, and *Stern*, Ge muttered to himself.

Chang followed the manual and pulled on his silk gloves, which he produced from one of his tunic pockets. Silently and quickly he took out a battery-powered scanner from his handbag and proceeded to methodically sweep in slow, spiraling geometric patterns every room in the house for hidden microphones and electric alarms.

Ge walked over to the Soviet upright piano in the living room and started looking at the mounted photographs. They were all family shots in various combinations of three, in keeping with the state mandate of one child per family—a man, a woman, and a boy of eight or nine. Picking up one taken in the outside courtyard, Ge tried to find in the father—the junk man most likely—some resemblance to himself or someone he knew. Finding none, he concluded that it was only an accident, a sheer chance of mathematical probability, random, that he was not someone in another life in one of these pictures, or that someone in his.

"It's clean," Chang interrupted Ge's thoughts with this assurance, and proceeded to search every room, notebook, and pen, specimen bag and latex glove in hand.

Ge went outside and lit one cigarette after another until Chang came out empty-handed, just as he was about to open another pack.

"Colonel leader," Chang started.

"Please be free of the unnecessary, especially in field work."

"Yes, perhaps."

"Did you find any sign of the enemy?" Ge asked, flipping the cigarette butt over the walls of the courtyard.

On his walk back to his apartment, Ge was beginning to wonder if he was losing his grasp on his own life, after spending almost that entire day with Chang. He tried to tackle this question piece by piece in the cold, explaining points to himself. His eyes would rest momentarily on those he passed in the street in the gathering twilight, wondering how much each one of them was willing to put up with and still remain in the country.

The familiar sound he heard was probably flutes. The animals and birds that he saw were probably dreams by the river, hazy in the gloaming and barely distinguishable from the landscape.

He hoped that Panda would not drop by this evening; he did not want to be seen by his friend in this exhausted, self-doubting condition.

CHAPTER SIX

And then what happened? What happened at Tiananmen Square? Was Ge a different person before June 4, 1989? Was there a single conspiracy, or in fact several competing conspiracies that exploded that night in Beijing? Had they always existed, festering just below the surface ever since Zhou Enlai parted the Bamboo Curtain in greeting President Richard Nixon when he stepped off Air Force One in Beijing in 1972? Or did they go back to 1912, when Sun Yatsen became the first president of modern China? Or even further back? Should they have been predicted, or were they random collisions in time and place to which ideologies were incidentally attached, along with the bystanders who invented them, killed for them, or died for them? And did Ge take a side? Did Ge, at 35 a colonel in the Ministry of Public Security at the national capital and chief steward of Beijing's political stability, did he have a choice, and did he exercise it? Did he take his six-year-old son to the Beijing Zoo?

The meeting had been going on ever since dawn. The competing candidates sat around the square table scanning their personal copies of the speech that was being read from the rostrum into the microphones at the front of the meeting room. Even though no one knew who wrote the original text, most of them were also taking notes of the speech for future interpretations of its subtexts and tucking them away into the little receptacles they had brought along. Television cameras from every major city were recording this meeting for a delayed news telecast following another late evening scene from the animal kingdom.

Finally the speaker departed from the prepared text, looked up and asked his audience, "Are you willing to accept this responsibility as defined by Clause 16 of Article 89 of the Constitution?" while the glare of the TV camera lights reflected off his glasses.

Outside the building, tanks and armored personnel carriers were being driven into position, ready to enforce martial law at the country's capital, engines running.

At 10:00 P.M. exactly on June 3, tanks and soldiers of the 38th Army started moving cautiously down Chang An Boulevard toward Tiananmen Square, most of the uniformed PLA soldiers under twenty years of age, unarmed and uncertain of the orders coming from the command post set up in the Western Hills outside Beijing.

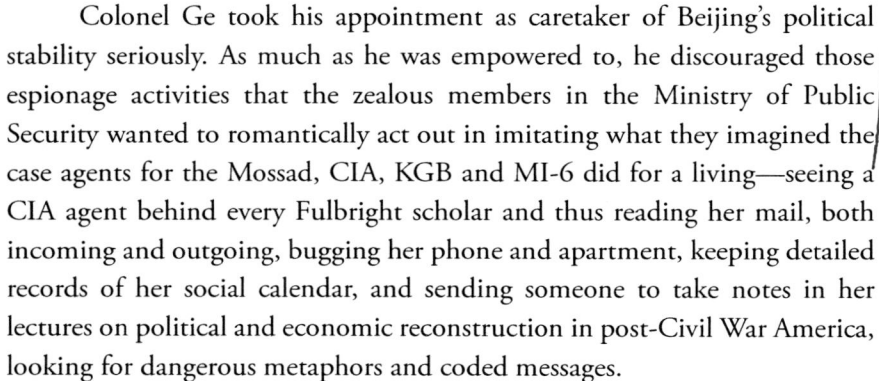

Colonel Ge took his appointment as caretaker of Beijing's political stability seriously. As much as he was empowered to, he discouraged those espionage activities that the zealous members in the Ministry of Public Security wanted to romantically act out in imitating what they imagined the case agents for the Mossad, CIA, KGB and MI-6 did for a living—seeing a CIA agent behind every Fulbright scholar and thus reading her mail, both incoming and outgoing, bugging her phone and apartment, keeping detailed records of her social calendar, and sending someone to take notes in her lectures on political and economic reconstruction in post-Civil War America, looking for dangerous metaphors and coded messages.

If nothing else mattered, his annual budget was inadequate for this kind of paranoiac surveillance activity, not to mention the storage problems in the ministry's six-block warehouse out on Fucheng Lu that was already bulging from uncataloged, untranscribed, untranslated, and uninterpreted tapes collected over the years from every foreign residency—be it embassy, hotel, or guest house in Beijing.

But this week was another matter. Ge had to finalize security arrangements for Soviet Premier Mikhail Gorbachev's state visit next week. Henry Kissinger's visit in early May was a simple matter, a relatively straightforward, nonthreatening itinerary in which he was pimping his political connections and representing his American business clients salivating over the immense Chinese market, a trip not even covered by CNN. There, it was naked money and nonsymbolic—Ge had only to make sure that the furs and ivory that Kissinger purchased remained safe between the hotel and the airport. But CNN has been here all week preparing for Gorbachev.

So Ge went undercover to test Beijing security, especially the crowded and vulnerable airport. Dressed as an anarchic, postmodern academic in jeans, soft black shoes, and with a wrist book bag, his normal walk changed—steps a little less strident and moving more from the knees than hips and toes; he first practiced it walking around the Soviet Embassy in the Sanlitun Compound. He tried to test his disguise on the foreigners he passed by, giving them as insulting a look as he could muster in his role as the nationalist activist: I don't give a shit who you are, Australian, Italian, Swedish, Canadian, or West German. You are all white and have the exact same colonial manner about you. But as he had expected, they were mostly diplomats bent on their foreign service careers and did not even notice him, buried in this bedrock of the Cold War.

At the airport Ge knew that he must try something more radical to test the security there. After changing into tennis shoes and picking up a shoulder book bag and American passport from the trunk of his car in the parking lot, he resumed his normal posture, movements, and manners, and walked up to the window on the left main floor that issued special passes to the airport's sterile areas.

"I want a pass," Ge said, confident of his best English.

Fortunately the uniformed man at the window knew no English and, not wanting to have anything to do with him—a foreigner, though he looked Chinese, maybe from Hong Kong or Taibei—turned away to look at the panda in the calendar on the wall. After Ge repeated himself in a louder and more frustrated tone, the man turned back to him and held up a small sign in Chinese, before noticing it and flipping it over to its English side: *I do not speak English. Go to information desk.*

Between the two young women at the Information Desk, they were able to understand that Ge wanted a special pass to the customs area to help his fiancée go through customs on her first visit to China, and whose flight from San Francisco was just landing at that very moment. Leaving their station unattended, they both accompanied him back to the Pass window and translated his request. The man pretended to look at Ge's American passport, and finally and reluctantly, for one *yuan,* issued him the green pass normally reserved for high-ranking diplomats.

Not so good, Ge thought; *this is pretty bad,* as he flashed his green card through several security gates and into the customs inspection area. Leaning against a railing and waiting for the passengers to deplane, Ge lit up a cigarette. A customs colonel with a walkie talkie walked over and in English checked out Ge's presence, but he was quickly satisfied when Ge showed him his green pass.

Moments later a young, perky woman officer with short hair walked straight up to Ge and without blinking, said to him in Chinese, "There's no smoking here. Who do you think you are? Even Premier Li Peng can't smoke here," pointing to the No Smoking sign.

Using the traditional language of containment, the scholars divided themselves into sects, but nevertheless claimed that the integrity of their academic objectivity prevented them from engaging in any political activity.

Fortunately for some it was still early, but for others, well, it brought on nothing but shame. Some of them will die early, and some of the others who might never die have no fear that they will be identified in any police lineup as the usual suspects that they really are.

Comrade Marshal Zhao is in charge now. Having distinguished himself in military campaigns against the Japanese Imperial Army and the Kuomintang's mercenaries, and having accompanied Mao on his 6,000-mile march to Shaanxi in 1934-5, Zhao was now impervious to criticism and could do no wrong. The last of the regiments had just moved into position, including the hard-core illiterate and older recruits in the 27th Army, many as a last resort to long prison terms. And now, seasoned in suppressing dissidence in Tibet, they were the first to be issued both AK-47s and live ammunition, even though many of their officers had not been issued Beijing street maps, and some did not even know that they were at the center of the Middle Kingdom.

In a few hours, the forty-year stronghold of attempted dominion over feudalism and corruption, hunger, homelessness and disease, chaos, the absence and abuse of dreams, subservience, plain everyday incompetence and stupidity, will completely break down around the Gate of Heavenly Peace. Ge's wife Xin Liu had been talking divorce more frequently this last month, too.

The Oroqens now number fewer than 500—they are all leaders, or former leaders, but most of them are widows of former leaders.

There are now more than 10,000 Oroqens. Since the government started helping them in 1951, six have graduated from college, sixty-four from technical schools, and more than two hundred from high school. Some of them have become teachers and government officials, and every year Oroqen singers, dancers, and storytellers travel to Beijing in October to perform in the National Day celebrations at Tiananmen Square in front of Premier Li Peng and state television cameras.

In equal numbers, the Muslims in China and the Mormons in Utah are being recruited for espionage work by their respective countries. They have until sundown to prove that their ecclesiastical war against rats, mice, locusts, and weevils can be appropriated for their secular war against wolves, bears, pigs, chickens, cows, horses, and other humans, albeit the Mormons had a head start on the first and the last in Nauvoo, Illinois, in the early nineteenth century.

At a display Oroqen's home, bear skins and a hunting rifle hang from the walls, and a birch bark canoe sits under the eaves. A color TV set, *Daffodil* washing machine, and *Panda* refrigerator dominate the traditional furniture.

This family has progressed from nomadic hunting, when bears and wolves were sacred animals, to the economics of farming and a little forestry. Rich now, and electric baseboard heating has replaced their traditional *kang* and they watch *Rambo 3* and *The Sound of Music* on their VCR in the evenings.

Just how does one start counting? Begin with the bodies, or finish with the bodies, or not include the bodies at all? Are all the bodies equal? And are all the bodies where they're supposed to be?

"Maybe we can wait for the number to be announced on CNN, or wait for the secret to be declassified and published by the State Statistics Bureau unless the next Red Guard gets to the numbers first."

"Secret, my ass. If it's published, then it isn't true. You should know that; we do the same kind of work here."

"Maybe we should wait for the world press?"

"What? You got to be kidding. They sleep in the same guarded and walled compounds as the diplomats, and they barely ever leave the embassies and the lounge of the Beijing Hotel where they trade rumors and corroborate with each other as independent confirming sources. Rely on them for accuracy? You've got to be kidding. Better to read a Lonely Planet travel guide."

"It does not matter; no one really cares."

Ge was listening to this conversation among several communications officers from the Public Security Bureau at the mobile communications center set up near the military airport, away from the sound of gunfire and smoke around midnight, when Comrade Marshal Zhao entered, preceded by two high-ranking Central Committee members and several staff officers.

"Colonel Ge." The Marshal Zhao walked right up to Ge without being introduced. "Under the circumstances, you must understand that we have to impose a different chain of command, I'm sure. Even I have to work directly with these two representatives," he added, pointing to the two Central Committee members who were looking away.

"I have been told that you are the only person in Beijing who can get some crucial information for us," he continued, loosening the top button on his tunic.

"Of course, I'll do my best," Ge said, already anticipating the question.

"You see, I have been told that you are the only one who knows the infrastructure in Beijing well enough to compile an accurate and reliable body count of the fatalities in this riot tonight. Is that correct?"

In the flash of a microscopic second between the question that Ge had anticipated and the answer, he was nevertheless still surprised by the directness of it—a fractional inattentive moment that was felt by Ge himself and will be remembered for the rest of his life, but which at the time went by unnoticed by everyone else in the room except the Marshal Zhao.

"No, sir," he lied. "That is not true. It's impossible now. Maybe in two or three weeks," he clarified, looking straight into Zhao's eyes, his universal denial uttered with as much inherent authority and adorned conviction that Ge could muster for this moment.

There was a longer moment this time, of silence not heard, not heard among the soldiers and students, policemen and thugs, workers and merchants, doctors and foreign journalists, all the way down to Tiananmen Square with tremendous consequence—this time there was no room for the storyteller to escape.

Alex Kuo

CHAPTER SEVEN

A humongous volunteer land army had been gathered by Mao Zedong between the end of World War II and 1948, and with fire, sword, and word he promised to obliterate all the forces of evil and suffering and establish China as a socialist nation state along selected Marxist lines. By the end of the 1949 summer, Chiang Kaishek was defeated and banished to Taiwan, at the very last minute absconding with all of the country's gold reserves, art treasures, and Steinway CDs stored in the Forbidden Palace, literally less than one hundred meters from where Mao's back was turned to it on October 1st at Tiananmen Square, proclaiming to one and all and Movietone cameras too that China was henceforth a unified and independent republic.

For the first time in history, all of China's immense political and geographical power had shifted into a centralized imagined community. For a spectacular moment as he stood there surrounded by thousands of red and yellow chrysanthemums at the front of the review stands between the lions in the newly minted capital of Beijing, Mao looked as if he finally involved himself in something that he could not get out of.

Xin Liu knew it was easier for her there in Beijing, where she had grown up, and though she wasn't worried about moving to Nanjing and facing the difficulty of making new friends, she did think about it a few times.

"I simply cannot continue to stay here in Beijing," Xin Liu confessed to Ge one Sunday afternoon while they were watching their six-year-old son in front of the lion cage at the zoo. "I simply must pursue my career path, now that there is that opening at the Nanjing television station. I must. Like that lion in there, I'm a prisoner here, and for what? If I had committed a crime, at least I would have reason to endure the acculturation activities, read poetry, or tend to the prison vegetable gardens or something."

The lion continued sleeping, above the endless spittle of clack-clack-clack-clacks aimed at it from little boys about Xiaonyao's age, their tiny fingers squeezed bloodless white around the triggers of their black plastic AK-47s.

"You know that I cannot request a transfer," Ge reminded her, having only recently and at the age of thirty-five been appointed by the party's central committee to watch over Beijing's political security.

"Yes, I know, I know," Xin Liu said, her voice lowered, looking away.

Xiaonyao left the company of the other boys with the weapons and wandered back to join his parents, reaching for his mother's hand.

"Perhaps we should continue discussing this tomorrow," Ge said, and reached for Xiaonyao's other hand.

Tomorrow, nothing will be different.

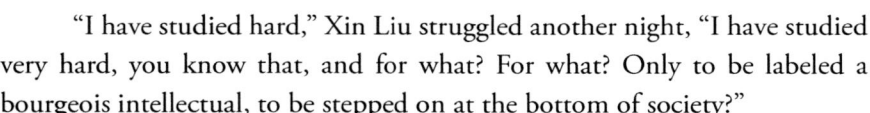

"I have studied hard," Xin Liu struggled another night, "I have studied very hard, you know that, and for what? For what? Only to be labeled a bourgeois intellectual, to be stepped on at the bottom of society?"

"Yes, I feel that heartache too," Ge answered, lighting up another cigarette and looking uncertainly at his wife.

Xiaonyao was tucked in for the night, and the two of them were gathered around the kitchen table, stroking the options and trying to take inventory of their chances together.

"In some ways you have been lucky," Xin Liu said, reaching across the table to enclose his hand with hers. "You have position and rank, and you have managed to get them without cheating or lowering your dignity. But you know damn well that sooner than later you're going to have to start paying some price, or accept the inevitable punishment.

"China has always needed a prisoner. You are too obstinate, just too obstinate to wear a mask, or too anarchic. Your early years with the Oroqens have done you in, same damn thing."

"And you?" Ge asked and pulled his hand away, lit another cigarette and offered Xin Liu a drag. "You, you decided to go into television!"

"Aha, there's the advantage," Xin Liu countered, puffing on the cigarette. "They don't know what they have got yet in television. But for you, in public security, at least our inherited paranoia about the dissolution of power, and the shifting and threat of the loss of power that's been central to the Chinese—if anything can be described as being Chinese at all over the last forty centuries—give us some sense of direction.

"You, you Ge, you are in sheep's clothing; they do not know what they have on their hands, except that they do know you are stupid enough to keep your word and do what you are supposed to do in your judgment, maybe most of the time, even when no one's looking."

"How can you say that?" Ge asked, a little startled. "How can you say that managing political power has been our central characteristic for the last forty centuries? What about everything else, like art, like language, and like culture?"

"Exactly," Xin Liu continued, handing the cigarette back to Ge. "That's exactly why art and culture had to be destroyed, because they were completely wrapped up in the feudalism of class and power. And language too, it had to be standardized, along with the novel. In the new nation they could not be allowed to go their independent ways, subverting everything."

"Do you really believe that?"

"No, of course not," she said carefully. "No, but I have to live with it."

And they do not believe. They do not believe, in a country of hard invented realities.

At a state banquet for foreigners, where the country's money is being wasted for no purpose, no purpose at all, Ge and Xin Liu were both here, but they were not here together. They had arrived separately at her insistence, leading separate careers, she said, his and hers, hers and his.

"There are so many extravagant banquets here," Xin Liu continued when they were dressing back at the apartment. "And they are trading their dignity for nothing, nothing at all, not even so much as hope."

"It's not all that bad, this negotiation of convention. This kind of favor trading has been our social cohesion for centuries, our glue. What is traded keeps the country on the right track. Look, look, would you please brush off the back of my tunic? Look, we've practically eliminated hunger and homelessness in a country of over a billion people, when only a short forty years ago they were endemic problems."

"Isn't there a more dignified way to do it?" Xin Liu asked, trying on another silk scarf in front of their shared mirror. "This way is the same as begging."

"But dignity is not an issue here. People just do it, for the longer goal. And none of it is personal."

"That's exactly the problem, exactly."

They had decided when Xiaonyao was four that they would attend those public social and political functions when their respective jobs required their attendance, but they would go separately rather than as husband and wife, so that each would not be trading or treading on the other's career. To this extent they had defined their independent professional directions, with no complications, no asides, no additions, no restraints, no I-am-married-to connections.

To their friends who knew them as a couple, they appeared as ridiculous secret lovers keeping their public distance from each other, deliberately ignoring each other's presence sometimes in the same small receptions. On several occasions they had even been accidentally introduced to each other by the unsuspecting host.

Steadying herself when Xiaonyao was born, his mother had said, "It's a good thing that the government has finally passed the policy that each couple is allowed to have only one child."

Ge had sensed that there was no safe passage out of this declaration, the three of them there for the first time in the same room and united by blood at least if not something else, too. So he asked, as carefully as possible, smiling at their newborn cradled in her arms, "What do you mean?"

"I mean, it's the most radical change that the communists have made, and it's probably a good thing. Look, look at how ugly babies are," she nodded at Xiaonyao. "They're like little pigs, pink little piggies, with piglet toes and pudgy piglet fingers and no hair at all."

So unlike all of the other parents they knew whose children were quick-witted but absolutely helpless if left unattended like little emperors or little princesses, they made a promise to each other not to spoil Xiaonyao, not to pamper him after he'd grown out of the crib so that he would not have to suddenly bridge infancy and maturity overnight when he entered into marriage or work or both; and they made a promise to their country, which appeared to cocoon their citizens as if they were incapable of looking after themselves or each other.

"Yes, and it extends into our world of work too," Ge added. "It's as if we have subverted the one-child-per-family policy by extending the family into the workplace. Mao has given us a consciousness and arrogance, an awareness that something could be done about our own history, that we don't have to be caged animals all the time, that disparities can be adjusted, that there may be some hope after all."

Xin Liu cleared her throat and said, "After that consciousness is raised, after the cage is opened, what do we do next?"

They were at the kitchen table again, smoking and discussing politics, their inclination toward talk welling deeper and deeper in this, their moment of crisis.

"We have always been like this," she continued. "Papa and Mama have always busied themselves with their children's education, employment, residency, and only until recently, even their choice of marriage partner. Except that now with communism, the state has become the parents, the work unit has become the parents. The administrative organization of feudalism with its elaborate but clear assignment of authority and obedience has morphed into this modernized age, even co-opting the one-child-per-family policy that perhaps it had invented in the first place to take over that final stronghold of choice."

"You know that you're saying the idea of individual responsibility does not exist in China, that it takes a call from the mayor of Beijing just to get a pipe fixed in our bathroom, don't you?"

Xin Liu smiled at Ge in this moment in which their minds were instinctively encircling the same dangers.

After a moment of silence, she asked, "You know what we're saying, don't you?"

"*Shemmer?*" Ge wasn't sure he wanted to explore this any further.

"We're saying either that we don't have communism here, or that we've got a crazy form of communism that's basically a variation of what we've had all along, except that the power of decision making has shifted from the immediate neighborhood to a centralized government. But the final result is still the same: no one has any responsibility!"

"And no one has any power," Ge added, too far into it to back out now.

"Yes, what we have is a kind of determined anarchy in which the self, through a basic subservience to the larger political order, through sheer will, will barge ahead to get whatever we want done *done*, until we run into something or someone else's agenda that obstructs us with a very impersonal *Stop, Hold it, Stop.*

"Look," Xin Liu stood up to emphasize her point. "Look, Ge," she said, her cheeks' light glow vanishing as suddenly as it had appeared, something only a lover would notice. "Look, we don't even look surprised when that happens; we don't even take it personally either. We simply turn aside and try to find another way to get done what we want. We have accepted that it's normal and nothing personal when we bump into someone or step on someone in the streets. We don't even look to see whom we have stepped on. It's not that it's so crowded here, which it is, but that's bullshit. It's because we have given up our personal space, along with any responsibility of power."

"Is that what's happening to our marriage too?" Ge was beginning to look ahead for both of them. "We've been talking like this for months. Has that already happened to our marriage and we don't know it? Or are we just babbling like children who don't know what we're saying because we haven't lived enough…"

"…we have lived enough to connect our words to our acts and other tests of reality," Xin Liu interrupted, sitting back down at the table, but still pointing her finger. "Of course we have, but then we haven't either. I don't want Xiaonyao's life to be ours lived over again!"

"And what's wrong with ours?" Ge was restless, anticipating the obvious conclusion. "And besides, does he have a choice?"

"We could shift things around a bit so that he'll appear to have one," Xin Liu looked to Ge. "Or is that too much like the inevitable metaphor for Cold War?"

"Xiao Ge," she shifted, using his familial form of address. "What do you remember of your childhood with the Oroqens?"

"The mountains, real air, the blue sky, overwhelming space, animals, and Paishan and Natall. Why?" Ge was both surprised and perplexed that he had omitted the death of his classmate.

"That is much better than the rest of us can remember of the Cultural Revolution. My memory is of broken glass, mud, weevils in the rice everyday, the bitter peasants and the more bitter intellectuals working by their side, and the constant, constant chill for three years."

Here she stopped and looked up at Ge.

"We are of that generation, you know," she continued. "We will one day inherit the responsibility for this country. Do you think we will do anything different in the twenty-first century, or do you think we'll just get by again and resolutely lay another metaphor on top of the sick one we've already got?"

First there were the political leaders of the work units who had to be informed. Next, there were the relatives, at least those on Xin Liu's side. Then past and current friends, and the post office. What credit applications ask for. Finally, there was Xiaonyao.

How do you tell a six-year-old that his parents who seem to love each other have decided to get a divorce? How do you tell a six-year-old that his parents who seem to love him have more important things to do in life than be with him? How do you tell your six-year-old that you're leaving him in order to shape your own political destiny? How do you tell a six-year-old boy that he will be living with his grandparents whom he had seen only twice in his entire life?

Is this when Xiaonyao first learned that pain never misses?

There are tombs of unknown soldiers killed in the line of duty in national capitals everywhere.

Are there tombs of known soldiers killed by friendly fire anywhere prominent?

Are there tombs of unknown soldiers killed in the line of duty by friendly fire anywhere?

Are there tombs of unknown animals killed by friendly tranquilizing darts anywhere?

Are there tombs of known animals killed by hunters in the line of duty anywhere?

Are there tombs of dead animals anywhere besides the pet cemetery in Beverly Hills, California, USA, where Trigger the palomino is buried, at least the most favored one?

What are the masks masking?

Are the eyes beginning to show through the masks?

Xin Liu will transfer to the Nanjing television station news production job, a promotion, to oversee the nation's industrial progress reports, and coverage of national campaigns against prostitution and litter, energy waste, and undesirable Western influences. Later she will move into producing documentaries of her choice, beginning with a half-hour special on the history of the Mongolian yurt, picked up for rebroadcast by the centralized CCTV. But her heart will be savaged.

Ge will stay in his Beijing appointment. He will live Tiananmen Square, and its masks and metaphors will be interpreted as avoiding ignorance, deceit, racism, and sexism where allegiances can be and are betrayed overnight.

Xiaonyao will live with his retired grandparents in Shanghai, write letters to his mother, and talk on the phone to his father every third day. Is this what China has to do to keep from being a whore?

CHAPTER EIGHT

"So Panda, Panda, my friend," Ge said to his mailman sitting silhouetted against the diminishing Changchun sunset framed in his living room window. "You're still smiling, ever since you got here four cigarettes ago. Smiling in this picture here, peering out of your cabinet of natural history at me with those quiet, knowing eyes as if I were the one who's stuffed and mounted. What gives? What's the good cheer, Cute Cute?"

"I'm smiling because you have changed," Panda shifted in his chair and lit another cigarette. "You've finally made a decision that will make you happy. You've left the war and come back to reclaim your own life."

"*Shemmer?*" Ge asked, determined to keep the good news to himself just a little bit longer, even though he knew that Panda already knew.

"I think we should go out and celebrate," Panda said, standing up.

"Rent a chauffeured stretch limousine with tinted glass windows, and drink Nine Star beer and, hah, hah, smoke Panda cigarettes you mean, and go dancing, here in Changchun? Do you remember what happened the last two times we went out for noodles?" Ge reminded him. "And I don't feel like putting on my uniform today."

"There you go again, the skeptical side, when it's the best news you've had in many, many years, even though you haven't told me what it is yet."

Panda ambled toward the door and turned the double latches. "Let's go," he waved at Ge with his light forepaw. "Let's go before you find another metaphor for this benign indifference you've adopted like everybody else since Tiananmen Square."

Some animals and some birds mate for life. The Carolina parakeet ties this knot one twist tighter. The entire communal flock will hover around its gunshot-dead member, ever waiting, even while the Audubons and the Wilsons are busy jotting down their body counts. For some others, blood thickens and is indivisible. Jane Goodall records mother gorillas pleading with outstretched, supplicant palms at departing helicopters from which string nets hang stuffed with their tranquilized offspring, destined for the zoos in Washington, San Diego, London, Tokyo, Beijing, Munich, and Paris.

How long did Sulin's mother wait for him while he was being transported to Chicago's Brookfield Zoo?

Did Ruth Hackness invent evacuation insurance without consulting Lloyd's? For Sulin? For her husband's body? For herself? For Ge and Xiaonyao?

Did Xin Liu feel such biological imperative? Or did language, poetry, and other forms of political metaphors that promised compensation for alienation effectively short-circuit such providence? What was she doing for her broken heart, there in the Nanjing TV studio? Was she just waiting, waiting, like everyone else just waiting, eyes without joy, steps without lift, nights filled with dead-end dreams, filling little scraps of paper with reluctant notes to herself?

"I know it'll be hard to explain this, Panda, my friend," Ge said, on their way to Xinlicheng Reservoir—their compromise. "But in my last year at Beida I petitioned to be a party member. As class monitor I was accepted immediately."

"I didn't know that, but you don't need to feel apologetic about it. In the 1970s, that's completely understandable."

"Aha, Panda, for once you missed it. I was going to describe what I used to do at about the time I joined the party."

Panda looked across the front seat at Ge, who appeared to be tentatively pleased with himself at this ongoing confession.

"Hey, I used to write poetry," Ge said, his eyes focused on the dirt road, the smile on the corners of his mouth twitching an apology.

"No, no, I did not know this about you," Panda said, trying to suppress his incredible laughter. "That certainly explains why you don't get any mail now," he added, before breaking down into uncontrollable laughter, tears rolling from his eyes.

"Yes, yes, very funny, but we're here. We are where we go," Ge said, turning off the engine and getting out of the car, relieved at the opportunity to change the topic that was getting out of control.

Panda ambled quickly along behind Ge as they walked around the reservoir in the late winter twilight. "You can't get off so lightly. What kind of poetry did you write?" he insisted.

Ge stopped so suddenly that Panda bumped into him.

"You want to know where you're going," he said, "or we'll both be rolling down this embankment onto the ice. And, hah, hah, I suspect even your fur isn't thick enough for that chill. Actually I did not write many, but I remember a very long one about abstract moods, sounds, and political unrest."

"All of that in one, *shemmer?*" Panda could not help it, but by now he was rolling in the frozen dirt, his laughter diminishing in the oxymoron the faster Ge tried to walk away to ignore it.

EXPRESSION

I will describe a mood
A white mood
That cannot talk
Whose presence you cannot feel

It comes from another star
And is here in this strange world
Only for one night

Such a long shadow
It trails in its distant beauty
What it cannot find is another shadow

Should you liken it to a stone
For icy reticence
I will tell you it is a flower
Whose scent rises on night air
Only to enter the plains of your consciousness
When you die

No music can realize this mood
Nor dance convey its form
You can never know how much hair it has
Or why it should comb it in this style

You love her and she not you
Your love started at the tail end of last spring
Why not at the dawn of this winter?

I will express a mood of cellular motion
I will consider why they rebel against themselves
And bring themselves stimulation and anger

I know the mood will be hard to express
Why for instance does nightfall approach now
Or I love her at this time
Or you die at this time?

I know that a trickle of blood is silent
And cannot for all its tragedy
Melt the steel clad world

Moving water makes a noise
A splitting tree makes a noise
A snake twining around a frog makes a noise
What then does the noise betoken

Preparation to transmit a mood
Or to express an inherent feeling?

Rather the weeping
The incommunicable weeping
China's sons and daughters have shed tears at the old wall

Thousands died in Hiroshima
Japan has shed tears before now
Those who died in a just cause
And those too timid have shed tears
As hard as it may be to comprehend

A white mood
An inexpressible mood
Has come to this world
Just tonight
And is beyond our vision
Quietly enveloping the entire universe
Incapable of diminishing or of leaving us
Unable to rest, unable to sense
Because we will not die
Because by moving, we make everything else move

In the extended phone call three days ago, Xiaonyao had asked his father how much longer the animals had to wait in the zoos, and he also said that he did not understand why they could not be together. Today, Ge's answer was clear and simple.

Ge finally stopped long enough to tell Panda that he was going to Shanghai to gather his son Xiaonyao from his grandparents, what they had decided in abundant joy on the phone this morning, and that they were going to start with a holiday, stopping at the Nanjing television station first.

Ge had decided to stop shielding himself from the truth of his own life, from what could cause him pain, and he took the chance, chose the trouble that was worth getting into, in the process leaving his country behind in his country. In all these years of protecting his country's security, he had also protected himself from the truth, believed in the same myths, adorned the same masks, kept out the same foreign influences however oppressive or liberating.

Tienanmen as public disturbance

"Then what will you do?" Panda asked.

Ge still did not know for sure: was Panda the messenger who has become his friend, or was Panda's presence in his life the message itself? But he could hear his heart beating, beating in the pandemonium of hope, and he did not stop to wait for the reason, fulfilled just to take his story one episode at a time.

CHAPTER NINE

By the end of the twentieth century some animal species have learned to make the adjustment between politics and environment. But barely a day passes that Ge does not look out his window without warning and remember to count the days left until the next time he will call Xiaonyao at seven in the morning as arranged. And barely a day passes that he will not think about the days in the mountains when he lived and worked with the Oroqens.

Each day he grew more impatient as he tried to move the emphasis between metaphor and ambiguity, occasionally stumbling in his language of radicals that added to, but took away more than it clarified. And each day he thought about taking up ink and brush to understand the fundamentals of expression and image. He would make his own ink rather than use one factory-produced, just as he had aimed at and killed the reindeer that he ate rather than rely on an anonymous butcher in the demilitarized supermarket.

Ge believed that most animals do not know any more than humans do, and are equally prone to making stupid mistakes. Their disadvantage is that sometimes things happen before they know it, and their advantage is that they are better at waiting. But how long can they wait for that cease fire? How long can they wait while their homes are destroyed, relatives maimed and killed, others kidnapped and taken prisoner, the dead tossed out and left uncovered in alleys, wild fields? At best they are placed in reserves, often belled and numbered, their eating, sleeping, and mating sequences tabulated and parlayed into dissertations, publications, or promotions.

When they left Shanghai together by train the next afternoon approaching nightfall, Ge and Xiaonyao quietly gazed into each other's traces. It extended farther, out of their sleeper into the gathering sheets of moonlight surrounding the passing countryside outside, and returned with their personal shadows of tremendous consequence, however slightly imperfect. Because they will not kill what they love most, they will not die, they will not die.

"Does your friend Panda know he got here?" Xiaonyao asked, sipping from his can of chilled coconut juice.

"Maybe not exactly, but he knows he took a chance in coming here," Ge said. "He's not timid, that's for sure. He'll meet us at Xian and show us that misty mountain country he grew up in."

"Can I call him *Cute Cute*," Xiaonyao asked, hugging himself and letting go a substantial smile, turning his head slightly toward the window.

"You'll have to ask him that yourself."

"Why?"

"I can't explain everything," his father answered.

From a turn in the tracks they could see the receding lights of the city, until the train straightened again, passing hamlets silhouetted in the steady moonlight, an occasional light flickering.

In their deep sleep they shaped their mouths that told them everything in their own language, their blood here too thick to bear what the country wanted them to have. So they stopped their waiting and took more, while their heart was still in one piece.

And so they dreamed. Sometimes, just sometimes, when the meaning becomes extravagant, life offers up a second moment.

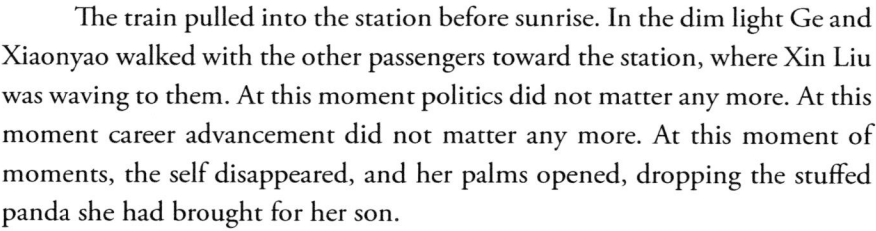

The train pulled into the station before sunrise. In the dim light Ge and Xiaonyao walked with the other passengers toward the station, where Xin Liu was waving to them. At this moment politics did not matter any more. At this moment career advancement did not matter any more. At this moment of moments, the self disappeared, and her palms opened, dropping the stuffed panda she had brought for her son.

THE ANIMAL GRAMMAR

Alex Kuo

He's an ALBATROSS

ALLIGATOR bait

ALLIGATOR tears

He's an ANIMAL

ANTs in the pants

ANTsy

PissANT

APEshit

He went APE

JackanAPEs

To APE

ASS backwards

Back ASSwards

DumbASS

Haul ASS

He's an ASS

JackASS

SmartASS

Stupid ASS

To BADGER someone

She's a BANSHEE

She's a BARRACUDA

BAT out of hell

BATs in the belfry

BATty

Blind as a BAT

DingBAT

Old BAT

BEAR ass

BEAR of a job

BEAR market

BEAR paw

Angry sow BEAR with cubs

Dancing BEAR

Does a BEAR shit in the woods

Honey BEAR

Snug as a BEAR in a rug

Strong as a BEAR

Sugar BEAR

Teddy BEAR

BEAVER

Busy as a BEAVER

Eager as a BEAVER

Crazy as a BEDBUG

BEEhive hairdo

Busy as a BEE

Making a BEEline

She has a BEE in her bonnet

Spelling BEE

The birds and the BEEs

Where's the BEEF

BIRDbrain

BIRDie

BIRD in bush

BIRD in hand

BIRD-legged

BIRD's-eye view

BIRDs of the same feather

BIRD song

Deader than a dodo BIRD

Eats like a BIRD

Free as a BIRD

JailBIRD

Kill two BIRDs with one stone

LoveBIRDs

Shit for the BIRDs

Sing like a BIRD

SnowBIRD

The BIRDs and the bees

The early BIRD gets the worm

A BITCH in heat

She's a BITCH

Son of a BITCH

The work is a BITCH

To BITCH

He's a BUCK

BUFFALOed

BUG-eye

BUG fucked

BUG off

Crazier than a June BUG

He's a BUG

LitterBUG

Put a BUG in his ear

ShutterBUG

Snug as a BUG in the rug

BULLdozer

BULL feathers

BULL in a china shop

BULLish

BULL market

BULL's eye

BULLshit

Cock and BULL story

Taking the BULL by the horns

Buckle BUNNIES

Gun BUNNIES

She's a BUNNY

BUTTERFLIES in the stomach

BUZZARD's roost

Old BUZZARD

Fatted CALF

Golden CALF

CAMELback

The straw that broke the CAMEL's back

Threading a CAMEL through the eye of a needle

Sing like a CANARY

To CARP

CATamaran

CATbird

CATboat

CAT (bulldozer)

CAT burglar

CATcall

CATfight

CATfish

CATgut

CAThouse

CATnap

Cat-o'-nine-tails

CAT rig

CAT's cradle

CAT's eye

CAT's meow

CAT's pajamas

CAT's paw

CATtails

CATty

CATty corner

CATwalk

CAT whiskers

CAT with nine lives

Alley CAT

Copy CAT

Curiosity killed the CAT

Fat CAT

Fight like CATs and dogs

Has the CAT got your tongue

Higher than a CAT's back

It's raining CATs and dogs

Let the CAT out of the bag

Playing CAT and mouse

PoleCAT

Quicker than a CAT on a hot tin roof

Skinning a CAT

TomCAT

Top CAT

He's a CHAMELEON

My CHICKADEE

CHICKEN

CHICKEN feed

CHICKEN-hearted

CHICKENshit

CHICKEN with its head cut off

Counting the CHICKENs before the eggs are hatched

Fox loose in a CHICKEN coop

Have the CHICKENs come home to roost

She's no spring CHICKEN

CLAM up

Happy as a CLAM

COCK and bull story

COCKeye

COCKshy

COCKsure

COCKtail

COCKy

Going off half COCKed

He's a COCK

PoppyCOCK

ShuttleCOCK

Crazier than a COON

He's a COON

Drunk as a COOT

He's an old COOT

COWed

COW-eyed

Cash COW

Holy COW

Sacred COW

Till the COWs come home

CRANE your neck

Sky CRANE

Jiminy CRICKET

CROCODILE tears

Crooked as a CROCODILE

CROW's feet

CROW's nest

As a CROW flies

Black as a CROW

Eat CROW

To CROW

CUB reporter

Sow bear with CUBs

He's a CUR

DOG-and-pony show

DOG days

DOG-eared

DOG-eat-dog world

DOG face

DOGfight

DOGgone

DOG Latin

DOGleg

DOG patch

DOG pile

DOGs of war

DOG soldier

DOG tags

DOGwatch

Ain't nothing but a hound DOG

Attack DOG

Crazier than a coon DOG

Dirty DOG

Every DOG will have its day

Feed him to the DOGs

Fight like cats and DOGs

FireDOG

Gone to the DOGs

Hair of the DOG that bites you

Hang DOGged

He's in the DOGhouse

Hot DOG

It's a DOG's world

LapDOG

Let sleeping DOGs lie

Lying DOG

Raining cats and DOGs

Red DOG

Salty DOG

She's a DOG

Tail wagging the DOG

Teach an old DOG new tricks

To DOG

Top DOG

Treacherous DOG

UnderDOG

WatchDOG committee

DONKEY

DOVEtail

He's a DOVE

Lovey DOVEy

TurtleDOVE

He's a DRAKE

DUCK board

DUCKies

DUCKing stool

DUCKpin

DUCK soup

DUCK tail haircut

Dead DUCK

Get all your DUCKs in a row

Lame DUCK

Lucky DUCKy

She's a DUCK

Sitting DUCK

To DUCK

Ugly DUCKling

Water off a DUCK's back

EAGLE

EAGLE-eye

Bald as an EAGLE

Spread-EAGLE

Slippery as an EEL

Memory of an ELEPHANT

White ELEPHANT

Wild as an ELEPHANT on the rampage

FISHing troubled waters

FISH story

A bigger FISH to fry

CatFISH

Drinks like a FISH

Going on a FISHing expedition

He's a FISH

It's FISHy

Living in a FISHbowl

Shooting FISH in a barrel

Swims like a FISH

FLEA market

Flea-bitten

Sent away with a FLEA in his ear

Die like FLIES

Drop like FLIES

Shagging FLIES

FLY in the ointment

FLY on the wall

BarFLY

Crazy like a shithouse FLY

Drunk as a FLY

Drunk as a FOWL

FOX guarding the henhouse

FOX loose in a chicken coop

Clever as a FOX

OutFOX

She's a FOX

Sly as a FOX

FROG in the throat

FROGmen

LeapFROG

Tall as a GIRAFFE

In a GNAT's eye

Within a GNAT's eyelash

Old GOAT

ScapeGOAT

Separating GOATs from sheep

That does about as much good as pinning a diamond on a
GOAT's tail

To get your GOAT

GOOSE bump

GOOSE step

GOOSE that laid the golden egg

He's a cooked GOOSE

Silly GOOSE

To GOOSE

What's good for the GOOSE is good for the gander

What's good for the GOOSE may not be good for the gander

Wild GOOSE chase

To GROUSE

HAM-handed

To HAM it up

HAREbrained

HAWKeye

HAWKish

HAWK nose

He's a HAWK

JayHAWK

To HAWK

HENpecked

Mad as a wet HEN

Old HEN

Scarcer than HEN's teeth

Red HERRING

HOG heaven

HOG-tied

HOGwash

HOG wild

Even a blind HOG gets an acorn sometime

Living high on the HOG

She's a HOG

Sweat HOGs

Whole HOG

Walking into a HORNET's nest

Madder than a HORNET

HORSE apple

HORSE around

HORSEfeathers

HORSE of another color

HORSEplay

HORSE pucky

HORSEpower

HORSE sense

HORSEshit

HORSEshoes

All the king's HORSEs

Beating a dead HORSE

Big as a HORSE

Bucked off a Belgium draft HORSE

Charley HORSE

Clothes HORSE

Dark HORSE

Eats like a HORSE

High HORSE

HobbyHORSE

Hold your HORSEs

Leading a HORSE to water

Look a gift HORSE in the mouth

Mind your HORSEs

One-HORSE town

Piss like a HORSE

SawHORSE

Stalking HORSE

Straight from the HORSE's mouth

Strong as a HORSE

Talking the hind legs off a HORSE

Trojan HORSE

WarHORSE

WorkHORSE

BoozeHOUND

To HOUND

Laughing like a HYENA

KANGAROO court

Frightened the KITTENs out of me

KITTY-corner

The KITTY

Gentle as a LAMB

Innocent as a LAMB

Leading a LAMB to slaughter

Sacrificial LAMB

An exaltation of LARKS

Happy as a LARK

It's a LARK

To LEECH

Change a LEOPARD's spots

LION's share

Feed him to the LIONs

Strong as a LION

To LIONize

Walking into the LION's den

Leaping LIZARDs

Crazy like a LOON

Holy MACKEREL

NightMARE

Richness of MARTENs

He's a MOLE in the CIA

Making a mountain out of a MOLEhill

Swift as a MONGOOSE

MONKEY around

MONKEY business

MONKEY house

MONKEY on my back

MONKEY see, MONKEY do

MONKEYshines

MONKEY tricks

MONKEY wrench

Drawn like a MOTH to flames

MOUSE around

MOUSE in the pocket

MOUSEketeers

MOUSEr

MOUSEy

Computer MOUSE

Drunk as a MOUSE

Playing cat and MOUSE

Quiet as a MOUSE

Quiet as a church MOUSE

MULE-headed

MULE pumps

Stubborn as a MULE

White MULE

Drunk as a NEWT

OSTRICH with its head in the sand

OWLish

OWLy

Boiled OWL drunk

Drunk as an OWL

Night OWL

Wise as an OWL

Dumb as an OX

Strong as an OX

PANDEmonium

To PARROT

Proud as a PEACOCK

PIGheaded

PIG in a blanket

PIG in the poke

PIG iron

PIG out

PIGpen

PIGtail

no word for
Panda
Trivialized
amusement

Bleeding like a stuck PIG

Guinea PIG

He's a PIG

In a PIG's eye

Sweating like a PIG

PIGGYback

PIGGY bank

PIGEONholed

PIGEON-toed

Clay PIGEON

Stool PIGEON

PONYtail

Dog and PONY show

Drink from a PONY

One-trick PONY

To PONY

PORK barrel

To PORK out

Playing POSSUM

Watch the POSSUM

PUG-nosed

Hush PUPPIES

PUPPY love

Lead around like a PUPPY

Mud PUPPY

PUSSY

PUSSYfoot around

PUSSY-whipped

He's a QUACK

RABBIT ears

RABBIT foot

Pulling a RABBIT out of a hat

RACOON's eyes

Separating RAM from sheep

RAT hole

RAT race

RATs

Drunk as a RAT

Cornered like a RAT

He's a RAT

He's a frat RAT

Not worth a RAT's ass

Pack RAT

River RAT

Sack RAT

To RAT

Round ROBIN

Packed like SARDINEs

Card SHARK

Land SHARK

Loan SHARK

SHEEP dip

SHEEP led to slaughter

Flock together like SHEEP

Looking SHEEPish

Separating SHEEP from rams

Wolf in SHEEP's clothing

She's a SHREW

He's a SIDEWINDER

SKUNKed

Drunk as a SKUNK

Slow as a SNAIL

SNAKE eyes

SNAKE in the grass

SNAKE juice

SNAKE oil

He's a SNAKE

Lower than the belly of a SNAKE

To make a silk purse from a SOW's ear

Eat like a SPARROW

He's SQUIRRELly

To SQUIRREL away

To give a bum STEER

SWAN song

Casting pearls to SWINE

He's a SWINE

Bloated as a TICK

Drunk as a TICK

TIGER eyes

TIGER on the prowl

Hold that TIGER

Paper TIGER

Put a TIGER in your tank

TOADying

TURKEY in the straw

Cold TURKEY

He's a TURKEY

Let's talk TURKEY

TURTLEdove

TURTLEneck sweater

Slow as a TURTLE

She's a VAMP

To VAMP someone

No good VARMINT

To WEASEL

That's a WHALE of a tale

WOLF baiting

WOLF in sheep's clothing

WOLF pack

WOLF whistle

Hungry as a WOLF

To cry WOLF

To WOLF down

Feed him to the WOLVES

Keep the WOLVES from the door

Can of WORMs

He's a WORM

He's a bookWORM

Lower to the ground than a WORM

To WORM

To YAK

PANDA HAS BEIJING BRIDEGROOM

Tokyo (Xinhua)—A ceremony was held at the Japanese Prime Minister Kiichi Miyazawa's official residence here on Monday to mark agreement on the exchange of giant pandas between China and Japan.

According to the agreement, Tong Tong, a seven-year-old female in Tokyo's Ueno Zoo, is to have Ling Ling, a male of the same age from the Beijing Zoo, as her bridegroom.

In exchange another four-year-old male, You You, also in the Ueno Zoo, will return to China. Photographs of Ling Ling and Tong Tong were exchanged at the ceremony. Ling Ling's was presented to the Tokyo metropolitan governor, Shunichi Suzuki, by the Chinese Ambassador to Japan, Yang Zhenya.

Visiting Chinese Communist Party General Secretary Jiang Zemin and Japanese Prime Minister Kiichi Miyazawa attended the ceremony.

Also at the ceremony a picture of You You, the younger brother of Tong Tong, was handed over to the Chinese Ambassador. You You was born in the Ueno Park in June 1988 by artificial insemination. His sister is now the only candidate for marriage. In order to avoid inbreeding, the Japanese authorities decided to choose a bridegroom from China and send You You back to its motherland, China.

At a banquet given in honour of Ziang Zemin shortly after the ceremony, Miyazawa said: "Only in this way can the pandas, the symbol of friendly relations between Japan and China, reproduce generation after generation."

China Daily, 8 April, 1992

About the
University of Indianapolis Press

The University of Indianapolis Press is a nonprofit publisher of original works, specializing in, though not limited to, topics with an international orientation. It is committed to disseminating research and information in pursuit of the goals of scholarship, teaching, and service. The Press aims to foster scholarship by publishing books and monographs by learned writers for the edification of readers. It supports teaching by providing instruction and practical experience through internships and practica in various facets of publishing, including editing, proofreading, production, design, marketing, and organizational management. In the spirit of the University's motto, "Education for Service," the Press encourages a service ethic in its people and its partnerships. The University of Indianapolis Press was institutionalized in August 2003; before its institutionalization, the University of Indianapolis Press published thirteen books, eight of which were under the auspices of the University's Asian Programs. The Press had specialized in Asian Studies and, as part of its commitment to support projects with an international orientation, will continue to focus on this field while encouraging submission of manuscripts in other fields of study.

Books from the
University of Indianapolis Press

(1992–2003)

1. Phylis Lan Lin, Winston Y. Chao, Terri L. Johnson, Joan Persell, and Alfred Tsang, eds. (1992) *Families: East and West.*

2. Wei Wou (1993) *KMT-CCP Paradox: Guiding a Market Economy in China.*

3. John Langdon and Mary McGann. (1993) *The Natural History of Paradigms.*

4. Yu-ning Li, ed. (1994) *Images of Women in Chinese Literature.*

5. Phylis Lan Lin, Ko-Wang Mei, and Huai-chen Peng, eds. (1994) *Marriage and the Family in Chinese Societies: Selected Readings.*

6. Phylis Lan Lin and Wen-hui Tsai, eds. (1995) *Selected Readings on Marriage and the Family: A Global Perspective.*

7. Charles Guthrie, Dan Briere, and Mary Moore. (1995) *The Indianapolis Hispanic Community.*

8. Terry Kent and Marshall Bruce Gentry, eds. (1996) *The Practice and Theory of Ethics.*

9. Phylis Lan Lin and Christi Lan Lin. (1996) *Stories of Chinese Children's Hats: Symbolism and Folklore.*

10. Phylis Lan Lin and David Decker, eds. (1997) *China in Transition: Selected Essays.*

11. Phylis Lan Lin, ed. (1998) *Islam in America: Images and Challenges.*

12. Michelle Stoneburner and Billy Catchings. (1999) *The Meaning of Being Human.*

13. Frederick D. Hill. (2003) *'Downright Devotion to the Cause': A History of the University of Indianapolis and Its Legacy of Service.*

For information on the above titles or to place an order, contact:
University of Indianapolis Press
1400 East Hanna Avenue / Indianapolis, IN 46227 USA
(317) 788-3288 / (317) 788-3480 (fax)
lin@uindy.edu / http://www.uindy.edu/universitypress

New Titles from the
University of Indianapolis Press

(2004–2006)

1. Philip H. Young. *In Days of Knights: A Story for Young People.*

2. brenda Lin. *Wealth Ribbon: Taiwan Bound, America Bound.*

3. May-lee Chai. *Glamorous Asians: Short Stories and Essays.*

4. Chiara Betta. *The Other Middle Kingdom: A Brief History of Muslims in China* (in Chinese and English). Translated by Phylis Lan Lin and Cheng Fang.

5. Phylis Lan Lin and Cheng Fang. *Operational Flexibility: A Study of the Conceptualizations of Aging and Retirement in China* (in Chinese and English). Translated by Phylis Lan Lin and Cheng Fang.

6. Alyia Ma Lynn. *Muslims in China* (in Chinese and English). Translated by Phylis Lan Lin and Cheng Fang.

7. James C. Hsiung. *Comprehensive Security: Challenge for Pacific Asia.*

8. Phylis Lan Lin, Editor. *Journey with Art Afar.* Catalog for the Au Ho-nien Museum, University of Indianapolis.

9. Winberg Chai. *Saudi Arabia: A Modern Reader.*

10. Philip H. Young. *Sandbox World.*

11. Mac Bellner & John Pomery, Editors. *Service-Learning: Intercommunity & Interdisciplinary Explorations.*

12. Rumen Gechev. *Sustainable Development: Economic Aspects.*

13. Chau Hang. *The Happy Brush: The Joy of Chinese Painting*

14. Alex Kuo. *Panda Diaries*

15. Christi Lan Lin. *Symbolism of Chinese Children's Bibs: A Mother's Affectionate Embrace* (in Chinese, Japanese, and English). Published by Les Enphants Co. Ltd and distributed by University of Indianapolis Press.

For information on the above titles or to place an order, contact:
University of Indianapolis Press
1400 East Hanna Avenue / Indianapolis, IN 46227 USA
(317) 788-3288 / (317) 788-3480 (fax)
lin@uindy.edu / http://www.uindy.edu/universitypress